MW00619917

ADVANCE PRAISE

Arizona Guy is good, clean fun. The mystery is believable and the characters and their surroundings even more so—Ray Spitzer has our hometown down pat. He stirs humor into the story, adds the seasoning of a little natural history, and pulls off a very readable first novel. I hope the next in the series is out soon so I can find out what happens next to my fictional neighbors.

~Gabrielle David, *Ajo Copper News*

Anyone who has wandered through Arizona's searing Sonoran desert will relate to Spitzer's description of the rocky, forsaken terrain and marvel at how a town as vibrant as Ajo ever survived—let alone thrived.

~Crismon Lewis Gresham, Ajo native and award-winning newspaper writer and editor

Raymond Spitzer's debut novel, *Arizona Guy*, is a charming, suspenseful mystery. Spitzer delightfully depicts the wonderful friendships and occasional dangers of small town life along the border between the United States and Mexico. With its snappy dialogue and captivating hints of potential romance between "Arizona Guy" Ted White & Detective Blanca "Sandy" Sandino, Spitzer's novel earns a well deserved place alongside other classics of the genre such as Robert Parker's *Jesse Stone* series.

~Rich Radford, (Torrance, California) *Daily Breeze*

ARIZONA GUY

by

Raymond Spitzer

WiDō Publishing • Salt Lake City

WiDō Publishing
Salt Lake City, Utah
Copyright © 2011 by Raymond Spitzer

All rights reserved. No part of this book may be reproduced or transmitted in any form or by any means, electronic or mechanical, including photocopying, recording, or by any information storage and retrieval system, without the written consent of the publisher.

This book is a work of fiction. Names, characters, places, organizations and incidents either are products of the author's imagination or are used fictitiously. Any resemblance to actual persons, living or dead, events or organizations is entirely coincidental.

Cover design by Don Gee
Front cover photo by Richard C. Spitzer
Back cover photo by Robert D. Spitzer

ISBN: 978-0-9830238-9-0

Printed in the United States of America

www.widopublishing.com

ACKNOWLEDGEMENTS

This project was developed over many years and required much sacrifice from my wife and children. I'm grateful for their unflagging support.

My editors at WiDō Publishing, Liesel Autrey DeVaul and Kristine Princevalle, helped me refine my vision. They held my feet to the fire and wouldn't settle for second rate writing. I'm thankful for their patience.

My brothers, Richard C. Spitzer and Robert D. Spitzer, shared their excellent photographs for the cover.

I'm grateful to Gabrielle David and *Ajo Copper News* for publicity and a bookstore in beautiful downtown Ajo.

DEDICATION
To my wife, Susan
the inspiration and love of my life

Chapter one

I didn't consider becoming an Arizona guy until I was called a California guy.

I drove alone out of Greenwood City, California, in my dark blue Toyota pickup, leaving behind its green lawns, leaves, and moss. I didn't realize how sick of green I had become until I found it growing in the back of my closet. Give me anything but green!

Ajo, Arizona fit that description, with its brown hillsides, black slag heap, white mine tailings, purple, gray, and yellow rock pile, gray-green cactus, and blue sky.

Having deposited my summer paycheck after checking out at school, I headed south. I felt both relief and anticipation. The relief came from being away from Janet Johnson, the woman who had warmed my heart before hers had turned as wintry as Siberia. Forget the cool fog of Northern California; I wanted the warm sun of southern Arizona.

I had accepted an offer to house-sit in Ajo for my aunt and uncle. I carried my contract for the next school year in Greenwood City with me, still unsigned.

At a gas station just off the freeway west of Fresno, I

overheard the clerk telling another customer about some local flowers. I wasn't interested, but when I paid for my lunch the clerk said, "Young man, you look like you could use some cheering up. Instead of going back to the freeway, turn right and go about five miles, just into those hills. You won't regret it. I guar-on-tee it."

Young man? I was twenty-eight. He was considerably older, bald, wrinkled, and had a large black mole on his chin. I was so depressed from brooding on the past that I couldn't summon up the energy to say anything. I nodded, paid, and left.

I didn't intend to do what he asked, but the traffic was so heavy that I couldn't get across the street to get back on the interstate. I fidgeted, fretted, and finally turned right, intending to do a u-turn when traffic permitted. However, once I was headed that direction, the hills drew me like a light attracts moths.

As I crested the first hill, I pulled onto the shoulder and sat in my truck, staring. There were flowers everywhere. There were also bushes and trees, but every square inch of ground between and around them was covered with flowers. I didn't know the names of any of them except the state flower, the California golden poppy, but their beauty awed me. I had never before seen so many flowers in one place. The colorful carpet continued as far as the eye could see, whites and reds and maroons and oranges and yellows and blues.

When I could breathe again, I got my digital camera and walked around taking pictures. I had no choice but to tiptoe on some of the flowers to get to a shady spot, where I could photograph the petals back-lit by the sun. This made the colors more vibrant and allowed me to use the silhouetted branch as a frame. I drove further into the hills, stopping here and there, caught up in the experience.

On the way back to the freeway, I returned to the gas station to thank the clerk with the mole, but he wasn't there. He must have gone off duty. That experience changed my entire outlook. I started looking to the future.

Getting off the interstate to avoid the Los Angeles traffic, I made it to Barstow, where I spent the night. I went right to bed and slept well.

The 'service engine soon' light had persistently lit up for the last hundred miles and was nagging again as I left the motel the next morning. I sought out a mechanic. The delay waiting for a diagnosis didn't bother me, but the verdict did. The mechanic said he was unable to get the proper recognition code from the truck's computer. He would have to replace it. Not having the computer in stock, he said he could get it from a place across town.

I pulled out my cell phone to call Aunt Betty and Uncle Bart while I waited, and found it was turned off. I must have neglected to turn it back on yesterday after leaving school.

The landine invited me to leave a message. I immediately hung up and tried Aunt Betty's cell phone. I got a recording which said, "The party you are calling is not available or not in the service area." Uncle Bart's cell phone gave the same message. That was odd.

The place across town didn't have the computer. It could be rushed in from Los Angeles, but I had to wait until morning.

I booked into a motel across the street and called Ajo again. The cell phones were still not available. I left a message on the landine.

I tapped out an e-mail message on my laptop and pushed send without much hope. Although I had gotten them set up with e-mail, Aunt Betty always said they were too busy to check it.

After downloading the pictures of the flowers from my digital camera, I had time to look for the names of the flowers on the internet. Poppies and lupine were the only familiar names. Delphinium, Eriogonum, and Monordella didn't mean much to me.

By the time the computer was installed and the 'service engine soon' light turned off, I had lost twenty-four hours. Now I was worried. The aftereffect of the singing flowers, which had given me a glow halfway the length of California, faded away and depression returned.

I called my aunt and uncle again from Gila Bend, forty miles north of Ajo, still getting no answer. High wind blasted the heat through my open windows as I drove the last stretch of highway. I poured drinking water on my shirt for short-lived relief as it evaporated. Within five minutes my shirt was dry. I tried it again but couldn't spare too much water. I was thirsty.

I passed a sign that said the Port of Entry in Lukeville was closed from twelve a.m. to six a.m. Another sign told me I was entering the Barry Goldwater Air Force Range, a bombing range for practice by pilots from Phoenix, Tucson, and Yuma.

Then I drove through a gap between two hills covered with black volcanic rocks. The sign said, unimaginatively, Black Gap. Paralleling the highway were railroad tracks which had not been used since the copper mine in Ajo closed.

Past Black Gap, white smoke billowed off to the right. I thought of a brush fire. Then I realized I was in the middle of bombing practice. Five F-16 jets circled the target, approached, and dropped their payloads, causing an eruption of white smoke every thirty seconds or so. They started their approach right over my head. I ducked. The smoke, flattened by the wind, blew away from the highway at an angle north and west.

A line of hills went from blue to purple to brown as I approached, with saguaros and craggy rocks developing. The moonscape of barren rocks and dust was called Crater Range, even though no craters were visible from the road. I glimpsed a hillside covered with saguaros and another cactus, quite a bit shorter, made of interconnected segments like sausage links covered with spines.

Emerging from Crater Range, I lost sight of the practicing jets. I could see Ajo in the distance, nestled under the next range of hills. One peak was decorated with a large whitewashed 'A.'

After crossing Ten Mile Wash I passed the turnoff to Child's Mountain. There were antennas and other installations on top, including a white tower with a globular top. It looked like a golf ball on a tee, except it was huge, dwarfing all other buildings.

The roadway suddenly seemed to end. Braking rapidly, I was engulfed in a fog-like white-out. I could no longer see Ajo, the hills, or even the highway.

Chapter two

The white-out continued with gritty particles crunching between my teeth despite my closed mouth, a sulfurous odor surrounding me. When I got below twenty-five mph, I could dimly see the edge of the roadway, so I steered by that until, suddenly, I emerged into broad daylight. The fog turned out to be a dust cloud boiling off the surface of the mine tailings, propelled by the fierce wind I had been battling.

The heat hadn't abated any, but at my slower speed the wind didn't blast through the window as fiercely and seemed a bit less hot. The word "cooler" could not be used in that context on that day. One could only say hot, hotter, and less hot.

Coming into Ajo, I passed a sign that said, 'Oasis RV Park,' and that made me chuckle. It was entirely brown, just like the surrounding desert. There wasn't even a palm tree. My previous visits had been in December when wall-to-wall RVs concealed how barren it really was.

Further down the street, parked between two trees that gave it meager shade, sat a huge blue RV built like a bus. It had psychedelic designs on the blue background as if a flower child had been let out of the 1960s. A sign in front said in neat lettering: Licensed Contractor, Locksmith, T.J. TATUM, Coolers/A.C. Whatever You Need.

Just past Pizza Paradise, I stopped at Bernie's Service Station before going to my summer home. The attendant took one look at me and said, "Just wait until summer really comes. This has been the coolest June I can remember, and I grew up in this town."

Glancing in the rear view mirror I saw that my skin was reddened, my brown hair tousled, and my dusty face streaked with perspiration. "Coolest June?" I thought. Spotting a thermometer, I couldn't believe it registered only 95°F. It had to be broken.

Stretching my legs, I noticed a boy pumping up his bicycle tire while whistling Bach. 'Jesu, Joy of Man's Desiring,' an anthem I used almost every year. He looked up, met my eyes, and smiled. Almost immediately he looked away, tending to his tire. He watched me with his peripheral vision, however, adjusting his position to keep me in view as I moved.

"Hello, I'm Ted White," I said.

The black-haired boy didn't respond. Then I noticed an earbud and a wire going to an MP3 player clipped to his belt.

While I pumped gas, the boy finished with his tire. He wheeled his bike toward me, pulling out his earbuds. He extended his hand and said, "Welcome to Ajo. I'm Marco Armendarez."

I stopped pumping for a second and shook his hand. He had a firm, confident grip and rough callouses. I said, "Glad to meet you. I'm Ted White. Are you in the school band?"

Then I mentally kicked myself. It wasn't like I could recruit him, but anyone who could whistle that well had to have musical talent. My habit of encouraging students to join band would have to be put on hold.

"Well, I *was* in the band," said the boy, his voice cracking. He had the beginnings of a mustache but hadn't shaved yet, though it wouldn't be long. "We don't know if we'll have a band next year. Dr. Wilcox quit, and it's been real hard to get band directors to come here. The school board may have to drop the program."

"I hope not," I couldn't help saying. "It's vital for learning. Did you learn 'Jesu, Joy of Man's Desiring' in the band?"

"Is that the name of it? I just thought it was 'Joy.'"

"Oh, you were listening to Apollo 100's version," I said. "I *thought* you were going a bit fast."

"You know Apollo 100?" Marco looked at the trumpet, clarinet, and flute cases in the bed of my truck with my luggage. He snapped his fingers, smiling broadly. "Are you interviewing for the band director job?"

"What makes you think I'm a band director?"

He looked pointedly at the instrument cases and then gave me a smirking sort of frown.

"All right, I'm a band director," I said. "But, seriously, I didn't know about the band opening."

"Now you do, and I'll put in a good word for you. My dad is the school superintendent." He mounted his bicycle, inserted his ear pieces, and started to ride away. He stopped, pulling out his earbuds again. "I'm getting pretty good on the trombone, if I do say so myself. I really like band, even if Dr. Wilcox... well, let me put it this way. If you can find your way to the school, you'll be a better director than he was."

He rode away on his bike, waving merrily, whistling once again.

I stared after him. There was no way I would seek a job here. My two December visits with high temperatures in the 70's and lows in the 40's had in no way prepared me for June.

I drove on to my aunt and uncle's house. The small ridge on the west side of Ajo contained three houses on the crest line overlooking the town. The closest was still painted white, but new desert landscaping made it seem more elegant than on my last visit. The tan brick middle house, my destination, had greenery that would do justice to any home in Greenwood City. The third was pale blue with landscaping dominated by hollyhocks and sunflowers.

The driveways were on the back side of the ridge. Getting there, I passed a hillside covered with the segmented, spiny cactus that I had seen in Crater Range. There were small trees with no leaves and green bark. Saguaros topped with large waxy white blooms towered over them.

As I came to a stop on a wide expanse of black gravel at the Ellsworth home, I could see most of Ajo. Several church steeples, a white dome, and an ornate bell tower showed above the houses. Beyond a cluster of palm trees at the central plaza, the white tailings dam stretched across the entire east side of town in front of blue mountains. The dust storm that had engulfed me was still in progress, but it no longer crossed the highway.

There was an expanse of luxuriant lawn beneath lots of trees surrounding the Ellsworth's large, tile-roofed home, but the flowers were wilting. Aunt Betty had once told me she didn't like automatic watering systems. Not only did they clog up rapidly in the alkaline water, she thought her plants did better with the personal touch. Besides watering and mowing, my assignments included keeping the pool maintained with chemicals, skimming, and vacuuming.

No one answered the door. There were no vehicles in the carport or on the gravel besides my truck. I wandered under the shade trees to wait, but regardless of the cool, green yard, the air was hot. Oppressively hot. Knocking on the back door yielded no better results than ringing the front doorbell.

Since the summer squash leaves were hanging from their stems like boiled spinach, I decided to start earning my keep. I watered the worst first, noting that the plants started perking up immediately. By the time I finished watering, even the squash leaves began showing some starch.

I would have turned the water on myself to try to cool down, except the water was hotter than the air.

The doors and windows were locked with all curtains drawn. Several sliding windows were open about three inches emitting cool air, but decorative iron bars effectively prevented me from even thinking of opening them.

Rock retaining walls on the east and west sides made the lawn level. Citrus, apricot, peach, and fig trees dotted the yard. The large vegetable garden was in back near the walled swimming pool.

Finding a padded bench in the shade of a chinaberry tree overlooking the town, I sat down. The hill sloped steeply to a white house with a red roof.

Uncle Bart and Aunt Betty were in their mid-sixties and in good health. They always went camping in June and hired someone to water. This year, a series of break-ins around town had prompted them to get me to house sit.

I tried calling both cell phones again, but they were still "not available or not in the service area." I grew somber and my eyes dropped to the rock wall. I saw a tiny black ant pop out of a hole. It was the tiniest ant I had ever seen. It was followed by another equally tiny ant, and then another. The line of ants stretched along the rock wall, down among the particles of cement, before disappearing over the edge. These ants were half the size of what I considered tiny ants, the ones that raided my kitchen for food scraps left beside the sink.

The heat crept back into my body despite the temporary relief of the deep shade. What could I accomplish in the middle of the Sonoran desert that I couldn't accomplish back home in fog-shrouded Greenwood City? The wind that had been present all day sped up, pounding me with heat, dust, and the loneliness of the moment. The locked house depressed me further.

Where were my aunt and uncle? They had planned to be here for a day or two so they could train me to care for the swimming pool and show me around.

Unable to sit still any longer, with one last glance at the tiny ants, I set off for the house to my right. A well-worn dirt path showed the way. This house was surrounded by swirls of different colored rock undulating around the green-barked tree, spiny cactus, and wand-like sticks covered with wicked looking thorns.

A large lemon tree was laden with half-grown green fruit with the characteristic pointed end. I reached into the foliage to touch one, scratching myself when I withdrew my hand. It had thorns like the other plants in this desert; they were just concealed better by the leaves. In contrast, the thorns on the green-barked tree were out in the open.

An inviting rush of cold air emerged as a white-haired Asian lady opened the door. Before I could open my mouth, she asked, "Do I know you?"

"Hello," I said. "I'm Ted White."

She looked puzzled, and asked again, "Do I know you?"

"No, but I thought perhaps the Ellsworths might have mentioned that I was going to house sit for the summer."

Another puzzled expression. "No, not a word. Well, no matter. You look hot. Come in for some ice-cold lemonade. I'm Gladys Takamine."

"Pleased to meet you."

Gladys didn't answer.

I was soon settled on a comfortable couch, tall glass of the best lemonade I had ever tasted in my hand, while Gladys sat in a rocking chair. This appeared to be her usual abode, surrounded by newspapers, magazines, books, and television. A grand piano filled half the room.

Gladys picked up the thin local newspaper and said, "Oh, I haven't had a chance to look at the paper."

Skimming the front page, she said, "Oh, no. Gary Wilcox has resigned. What will the school do for a new band director?"

"I heard about that from Marco Armendarez," I said.

Gladys ignored me, opening the paper wide. "Ah, the County Chronicle," she said. Then she laughed and read, "'Investigated disturbance on Ocotillo Street. Turned out to be twelve javelinas.'"

She continued perusing the paper, making occasional comments. "Oh, not again. 'Six UDA's transported to

Sells Hospital suffering from dehydration.' At least none died. Something needs to be done about that."

She turned to the last page. "Well, well. They're showing movies at the Plaza Theater again. I remember when that was the social event of the week." She folded the paper and put it down.

I cleared my throat and asked if she knew where Betty and Bart had gone.

Gladys looked up as if she had never seen me. "Do I know you?"

"We just met. I'm Ted White, come to house-sit next door."

"Oh, I'm sorry. I don't remember. I'm Gladys Takamine. Would you like some lemonade?"

"No, you just got me a glass." I lifted it and took another refreshing drink. What was wrong with her?

"Let me get you a refill." She went back into the kitchen without taking my glass.

This time I heard her voice speaking, but I couldn't make out the words. She returned without the promised lemonade and sat in her rocking chair. She said, "Oh, I haven't had a chance to look at the paper."

She picked up the Ajo Weekly Miner, again. "Oh, no. Gary Wilcox has resigned. What will the school do now for a band director?"

Many of her comments were the same as the first time, but she added several. "How can the utility company have let so many streetlights get in such deplorable condition? They don't even have power to them? Well, I never! But who thought up the name 'Project Dark Sky?' That's ridiculous. 'Gas prices are up.' This is news?"

She put the paper down. This time I remained quiet,

but Gladys looked at me, puzzled, and said, "Do I know you?"

"Yes," I said. This was getting spooky.

She wrinkled her forehead. "I'm sorry, I can't place you."

"Ted White. I'm here to house-sit next door. Remember, I'm looking for the Ellsworths?"

"I'm sorry, I don't remember. I'm Gladys Takamine. Would you like some lemonade?" Without waiting for an answer, she got up.

At that moment a car jerked to a stop in the driveway. Gladys changed course and opened the front door. Two police officers stood there. One, a stocky redhead, said, "Mrs. Takamine, are you okay?"

Gladys stopped in confusion. "What are you doing here?"

"Ma'am, you called us," he said.

She looked bewildered.

The other officer, a compact Hispanic with a neat black mustache said, "Does it have anything to do with the man sitting on your couch?"

Gladys edged outside with the officers, but I heard her distinctly. "Officer, who is he?"

Leaving Gladys outside, both officers entered, wary, hands held near their tasers. I sipped my lemonade calmly and said, "Hello, Officers."

Chapter three

I said, "I just arrived from California to house sit for my aunt and uncle, the Ellsworths, who live next door. They were supposed to be here, but they're not. They didn't answer their phone yesterday or today. I just came over here to see if Mrs. Takamine knew anything about their whereabouts."

The tension in the room eased, and the officers moved their hands away from their side arms.

The redhead, Deputy Jacob Weber according to his name plate, talked outside with Gladys. The deputy with the mustache, Pedro I. Mendez, stayed with me. He stood at attention. His uniform fit like a second skin, every crease neatly ironed, revealing his body-builder muscles.

"I think something is wrong with Mrs. Takamine," I said.

Mendez bristled as if I had attacked his integrity. "That is obvious. We were only able to respond because we have enhanced 911. Mrs. Takamine couldn't tell the dispatcher why she needed an officer or where to come." He keyed up his radio. "7-7-7."

A female voice radioed back. "7-7-7."

"Send code 901 to do a welfare check on the 10-17."

Soon two ambulances arrived and the medical technicians began checking Gladys Takamine's vital signs.

I walked out with Officer Mendez. "Do you have any ideas where the Ellsworths have gone?"

Mendez shook his head, not deigning to answer. Overhearing, one of the EMTs, a blonde, blue-eyed, slender female said, "I think they were supposed to leave on vacation yesterday or today." She looked enough like Janet Johnson, my former fiancée, to make me look twice.

Unlike my first encounter with Janet, however, I was not tongue-tied and didn't stare. Whatever it was that had attracted me to Janet, this EMT didn't have it.

I explained I had been delayed by car trouble in Barstow, but my aunt and uncle wanted to spend at least a full day with me, teaching me to care for the pool.

Mendez looked down his nose at me, the corners of his mouth tightening into a frown. He spoke quickly, like flicking a fly off his nose. "Have you checked around town? How do you know they're not out shopping or something?"

Not waiting for me to reply, he yanked open his patrol car door, got in, and slammed the door shut in my face. He drove off spitting black gravel, talking on his car radio.

I shook my head, wondering what I had done to upset him. Or was he just a jerk?

When the ambulance personnel completed their assessment, the blonde EMT said, "We'll be transporting Gladys to Phoenix."

"Isn't there a medical facility in Ajo?"

"Only a clinic. She needs a CT scan, and they can't do that here."

"What do you think is the cause?"

She hesitated. "There are several possibilities. We're getting several of her friends to come and sit with her husband. He's an invalid."

I nodded. "I wonder if he would know if the Ellsworths left a message for me."

She shook her head. "Doubtful. He mostly lives in a world of his own. It's difficult to communicate with him in the best of times, but he's asleep right now. I just checked his room."

She left in the ambulance with Gladys Takamine.

I wandered back to the Ellsworth's house. Still no one home. I looked at the pool. Since the wrought iron gate was locked, I had to climb over the brick wall. I was tempted to plunge into the oval pool, clothes and all, but I resisted.

As I came back over the wall, a man was working at the blue house with the flowers. I hurried to the chain link fence to talk to him, but was too late. He disappeared around the far side of the house.

I returned to my truck, deciding to drive around Ajo and look for my aunt and uncle. After burning my hands on the steering wheel, I found some yellow leather gloves in the tool shed attached to the carport that fit snugly like driving gloves.

I drove toward the mine. The road climbed a small hill from which I looked at a large white building crowning the ridge ahead. On my first visit to Ajo the slope below the mansion had been dotted with cement foundations, the remains of World War II era barracks. Now, neatly landscaped modular homes took their place.

The whitewashed "A" I had seen from this side of Crater Range was up the slope to my right. I turned onto Indian Village Road which took me between the Greenway Mansion and the open pit.

Stopping at the mine lookout, I got out and gazed into the pit, two miles across and six hundred feet deep. Except for the terraces, roads, and digging marks, this was the crater that should have been in Crater Range. Once upon a time railroad tracks had wound down to the bottom, but they were long gone. The wind seemed worse at the edge of the pit, but the deep turquoise-blue lake in the bottom appeared motionless. A bird glided into the depths of the crater, cruising down in a long, slow spiral. Everything else was still and silent.

I imagined the mine in full operation, trains running up and down, trucks hastening along the roads, drill rigs boring holes, men planting charges, blasts shaking the town, and loaders dumping the loosened rock into ore cars.

Most of the people who worked the mine were gone. The only ones remaining were those like Uncle Bart who had retired, along with a skeleton staff to maintain the property.

Aunt Betty had said there were periodic rumors that the mine would reopen—there was still ore well-buried—but nothing had come to fruition. I found the chasm both awesome and lonely. It had supported tens of thousands of people, provided thousands of tons of copper and other metals for industry, and now it lay abandoned. Since I was the only one here, it appeared that few Ajo residents came to pay their respects.

The Greenway Mansion, a long mission-style home, was much closer to me now than when I had first seen it. The paint was blistered and peeling. It appeared to be forsaken like the mine. An American flag, snapping in the wind, flew from a tall pole set on a knoll in front.

Indian Village Road descended steeply past the old hospital, a rambling vacant building with a weedy parking lot. Back on level ground, I continued toward the Plaza behind a red pick-up with three teenagers sitting in the back. I kept a lookout for the green Lexus that Uncle Bart drove.

The Plaza itself was a garden spot in the middle of the desert, with green grass, a double line of palm trees around the perimeter, and a healthy assortment of shrubs. It had an arched Spanish colonial style colonnade fronting three sides. The fourth side was graced by two white churches, one with the white dome I had seen from the hill.

After failing to find the Lexus, I parked on the north side of the Plaza and walked past the pharmacy, government office, theater, eye doctor, and post office.

Across the east side was the old depot, the signage still saying Tucson, Cornelia, and Gila Bend Railroad. I knew about Tucson and Gila Bend, but I had never heard of Cornelia. And where was Ajo in the name? The railroad started right here in Ajo.

When I reached the door of the depot I found an ice cream shop called The Milky Whey— 'Out of This World Ice Cream and Deli.' I was tempted. The rush of cool air as someone left convinced me to take a break.

A slender high school girl smiled and asked what I would like. The menu started with Sirius Chocolate and went downhill. I settled on Mars-mallow ripple.

When she handed me the cone, I said, "Have you seen the Ellsworths around today?"

"Oh," she said. "You must be Mr. White. Marco told me you might be our new band director. I play the flute."

It took a few minutes to establish that she hadn't seen the Ellsworths since last week, but she suggested Mrs. Gabinski at the real estate office. "She knows everything about everybody."

That interchange loosened my tongue and I asked around in Ajo Gift Gallery, a store that sold locally produced art. The clerk didn't know where the Ellsworths were but said, "They're our best customers."

I had no luck in the café or library either.

Finally a stooped, gray-haired man with a hearing aid said, "I saw them not twenty minutes ago over by the hardware store."

"Great!" I said. "Do you think they've gone home?"

"Yes."

"Were they driving their green Lexus?"

"They were on foot. They live next door in the trailer park."

My soaring hopes plummeted. "I don't think we're talking about the same people."

"Sure we are. Beth and Barney Welser."

I caught Mrs. Gabinski as she locked the real estate office. She said, "Oh, yes. Oh, yes. I'm sure Betty and Bart are still here. They have all sorts of things planned to do with you. I offered to have my yard service take care of their place, but Betty was adamant that she needed a house sitter. Just adamant. Yes, they're still here. Sure to be. Oh, yes."

She hadn't seen them since Sunday.

Back in my truck, I went through the only stoplight and meandered around town. I noticed an industrial plant processing the black slag heap, the high school with freshly clipped lawns, tennis courts, and baseball field baking silently in the hot sun, the sheriff's department, and a swimming pool in a large park, teeming with children.

Winding through a residential area I came across a large, burnt orange brick building with vertical white panels and a prominent steeple— the Mormon Church. Since my relatives were members here, I checked inside. A group of men played basketball on a carpeted indoor court. They said they would call my cell phone if they learned anything.

I drove past the health clinic, but there was no green Lexus. Several ambulances were parked at the rear of the building. When I reached the highway I had come full circle and was practically back at the Plaza. I turned the other direction, meeting the red pickup with the three teenagers seated in back coming toward me. Soon I was back in the business section with Bernie's Service Station and Pizza Paradise that I had passed through earlier. I looked at parked cars and people. No green Lexus. No aunt or uncle.

I entered Ajo Food and Drug and talked to the clerk at the information counter. The dark-complexioned lady looked up from the computer, focusing on me over her half-frame glasses. She said, "Betty comes in every Friday like clockwork. Bart never shops. I expect I'll see her day after tomorrow."

"Did you see her last Friday?"

"Wanda," she called over my shoulder, "don't do that now. Didn't you notice we need a bagger?" She shook her head. "New help. Last Friday? I saw Betty, but I didn't talk to her."

"Well, I'm here to housesit—"

"Oh, that's right. They're going for the summer. What'd they do, leave before you got here? Couldn't wait to hit the stream?" She laughed and slapped her knee.

The phone rang. She said, "I'll watch for them," as she scooped up the phone.

I got out.

I stopped for a quick hamburger, taking the opportunity to ask about the Ellsworths. The clerk, a young, rotund Native American, couldn't place them, but the middle-aged cook said, "You know, the man who gives the citizenship college scholarship."

"Oh," said the clerk, "the one Yadi won. I liked him, but I haven't seen him lately."

The cook hadn't, either.

While I waited for my order, a Native American wearing a red shirt and blue jeans walked up to the window. He looked familiar. I opened my mouth to address him as he stepped back, but before I could get a word out I was called to pick up my order. He had disappeared by the time I had collected my food and paid.

I drove up behind the red Ford Ranger once more. Only then did I realize the bed was filled with water, like a swimming pool. The boys were splashing each other, water sloshing onto the street. One of the teenagers had a curly red beard, one a green ball cap with curls showing from underneath, and the other straight black hair.

The sun was setting when I returned to the Ellsworth home. All doors were still securely locked.

A full moon was rising above the mountains beyond the tailings dam. Transfixed, I sat on the comfortable bench under the chinaberry again. The moon was brighter at the edge and had irregular darker patches, like continents, in the middle.

I watched the stars wink into sight as the sky darkened. When it was fully dark, the stars were twinkling and alive. I felt in tune with the infinite, much like I felt among the singing flowers, until a siren brought my attention back to earth.

I caught sight of the flashing lights of an ambulance as it wound through town and disappeared behind the mine tailings, heading toward the reservation. With the louder sound dwindling, I became aware of other noises which were as clear as voices from a boat on a frosty morning on Mirror Lake. A car engine roared briefly as if the gas pedal was floored. Voices and music floated up from the car wash. The clear high notes of a flute came from somewhere close. I wondered if it was being played by the girl from the ice cream parlor. Even closer, a bird whooshed past the light on the power pole, getting a handy meal of flying insects.

That drew my attention toward the pool, where a large owl sat on the wall. When it lifted off, it made no sound, despite having a wingspan many times that of the small insect-catcher.

Crickets chirped everywhere, faster than I ever heard before. I had read that the hotter the temperature, the faster crickets chirped. Ajo was hot enough that I pictured a cricket's legs rubbing together so fast they started smoking.

Then I heard a coyote's howl, just one, from the far side of the canyon behind me. In response isolated dogs began to bark.

Dogs! Where were the two dogs I was to care for? Why hadn't I thought of that before? Why hadn't they barked when I rang the doorbell? I tried the doorbell again. Deep inside I could make out the ring. No barking.

Three times in a row. No barking. Perhaps that was the answer. Had one of the dogs taken ill? Been bitten by a snake? Been involved in an accident? Where was the nearest veterinarian?

I strode back to the Takamine residence, hoping also that Mr. Takamine was awake and could answer questions. The living room lights were on, and the door opened with an inviting rush of cool air again, revealing a tall blue-haired lady. "Let me guess," she said, "Ted White."

She invited me in, but there was no sign of Mr. Takamine. She thanked me for getting help for Gladys. "When I relieved Cal Pinegar he said you might come by, but it's too soon for any update on Gladys."

I explained about my missing relatives and then asked, "Is there a local veterinarian? I wonder if something happened to the Ellsworth's dogs and they had to get veterinary care."

She considered a moment. "Betty doesn't care for the vet who comes to Ajo once every two weeks this time of year, so she goes to one in Phoenix." Seeing my hopes rising, she hastened to add, "But I don't know which one."

She agreed to let me make some phone calls to see what I could find out, and she showed me to a desk with phone and phone book at hand. I used my cell phone for the long distance calls. For the next half hour I heard "call in the morning" phrased more ways than I thought possible. Veterinary answering services were no help.

"What about Bart's and Betty's friends?" I asked.

The tall lady gave me a few names to get me started, and I asked each one who couldn't help me to suggest other friends. I kept a list to avoid bothering people more than once. There was no shortage of people to call, but I gave up after an hour of no new information.

I returned to the Ellsworth home. The full moon, now looking smaller but brighter than when it rose, gave me plenty of light to set up my small backpacking tent. I had tossed it in for the trip, thinking I might camp along the way.

Lying on my bedroll, perspiring freely, unable to sleep, I wondered how the first miners to this region had managed to survive. Ajo made Greenwood City seem heavenly by contrast. In fact, one day's experience had shown me that I belonged in Northern California. I could endure ten Janet Johnsons before I would live here. Tomorrow I would phone my principal, sign the contract, and mail it off. That decided I still couldn't sleep. It was too blamed hot.

At length, I got up, climbed over the pool wall, turned on the lights, and went for a refreshing swim. I was disconcerted by the first few bats swooping toward me, but I soon ignored them and for the first time in weeks really enjoyed myself. When my body temperature was low enough, and I had swum myself to exhaustion, I lay down on top of my bedroll in the tent and at last went to sleep.

A faint sound on the breeze roused me. It was still dark, but something was amiss. Crawling out of the tent, I noticed a flash of light from inside the house, somehow reflected around one of the curtains. Someone was inside.

Chapter four

My first impulse was to go after the intruder. Pulling on tennis shoes without tying them, I sprinted toward the front door. It was ajar. Perhaps my aunt and uncle had returned, but there were no cars beside my truck. Feeling it might be too dangerous to enter, I dived into my tent and got my cell phone. I dialed 911.

The operator said, "911, what is the location of your emergency?"

"240 North Rosedale."

"What are you reporting?"

"A burglary in progress. Someone is inside right now. There's a light inside, like a flashlight, and the front door is open. "

"Your name, please?"

"Ted White."

"Phone number?"

I told her.

"Is the burglary at the Ellsworth residence?"

"Yes. I'm here to house sit."

"I'll send officers right over."

I thanked her and hung up. I rushed back toward the

door, still hoping to tackle the intruder when I saw two sets of flashing lights speeding to the rescue. With help so close, I decided to wait by the gravel.

Officers Mendez and Weber were out of their cars and sprinting toward the house before I could say anything to them. The pair radiated such an aura of dominance that I stepped back. Deputy Mendez gave me a piercing look as he ran past.

Mendez took a position where he could see the front door and the sliding glass door on the town side, while Deputy Weber headed toward the back door.

Staying out of their way by the gravel, I heard Mendez's radio crackle. "7-7-7,

7-9-8."

Mendez said, "7-7-7."

His partner said by radio, "Back door is wide open. Tracks lead to the north fence."

Mendez said, "10-4. Let's clear the house first." He spoke calmly into his radio, but cursed when he finished transmitting and sprinted toward the back door.

Shortly the front door opened and Mendez came out, switching on the porch light. "He's gone," he said to me. "Tell me what happened."

He produced his notebook, stood rigidly straight, and made notes as we talked. He was still wired for action. His pen nearly ripped his notebook each time he wrote.

"I was sleeping in my tent when something woke me. I think it was a sound, but I'm not sure. I saw a light inside, in the office."

"Did you see anyone?"

"No."

"Did you go in the house at all?"

"No."

"How do you know the light was from the office?" His eyes narrowed as I answered.

I slowed down. I was a suspect here. Deputy Mendez didn't know me. If I said the wrong things, no matter how innocent I was, I might find myself behind bars. He had brushed off my earlier concerns. "I'm sorry," I said, "that was the office the last time I was here. It may have been moved, for all I know."

"How long ago were you here?"

"About three and a half years."

"How long had you been asleep?"

I glanced at my watch. It was after midnight. "More than two hours."

"Do you recall any sounds while you were in the tent?"

I shook my head. "Once I got cooled off swimming, I went into a deep sleep. I don't remember anything."

"When did you last check the doors?"

"Right before I went to bed."

"Tell me what you did yesterday after I left."

I told him about my tour of Ajo, mentioning the Native American I might have seen three times. Mendez said he was sure all three were the same person, Manny Molina. I said I had seen a red Ford Ranger three times.

He said, "That would be Steve Paasch, Lorenzo Carrillo, and Juan Rios." He wrote their names.

I mentioned meeting the basketball players at the church, but I couldn't come up with any descriptions.

"It doesn't matter," he said. "They're all off-duty sheriff's deputies and Border Patrol agents."

I also told him about meeting Marco Armendarez. Mendez rolled his eyes and didn't write his name.

I said, "Then I called veterinarians, thinking something might have happened to my uncle's dogs. I also called people who know my aunt and uncle." I stopped, reaching for my back pocket where I had stuffed my list. It wasn't there, because I was now in my light summer pajamas. "I have a list in the tent."

Deputy Mendez told me to get it. I dressed in the tent while he studied the list. "You have been busy," he approved, inviting me into the house. He didn't give me any clue as to what he had found inside, but he said to look and not touch, as if I was five years old.

The house was quiet as an empty church. The front door opened on a carpeted hall decorated with potted plants and framed paintings showing desert landscapes. Each painting had a typed card centered underneath. I glanced at them as we walked into the house, noting how realistic they appeared. There had been paintings in the hall on my last visit, but I only remembered one, the largest at the far end of the hall. It showed a beautiful desert garden backlit in front of an impressive cliff. Just in the right place to capture the eye was a hole in the rock with a trickle of water forming a long, thin waterfall. The cliff was detailed but in shadow, while the thin stream and numerous droplets of water were highlighted in full sun. The card said, "*Hole in the Rock* by Shibasaburo Takamine."

At the end of the hall, doorways opened into a bedroom and the family room, both immaculately clean and tidy.

The hall ended in the living room, which had another assortment of paintings, mainly portraits. Suddenly I came face to face with my mother and father. The painter had brought them vibrantly into life looking into each other's eyes, lost in love, just the way I had felt about Janet Johnson. I felt a little envy for my father because he had found something I had lost.

I realized that I looked a lot like my father, with the same low hairline, brown hair with a slight wave, white but easily tanned complexion, straight nose, blue eyes, and rounded but strong chin. His ears were the major difference between us. His were large and had prominent lobes, "noble lobes" he called them. Mine were smaller with short lobes like my mother's.

Deputy Mendez had stopped at attention. Didn't he ever relax? He asked, "Who are they?"

"My mother and father," I said. "I've never seen this painting before."

"Do they live in Ajo?"

"No, my father died and my mother now lives in Pennsylvania. I didn't even know this painting existed. I wonder who…?" I looked at the card beneath the picture and read, "*Everlasting Love* by Shibasaburo Takamine."

With an awkward, impatient movement, Deputy Mendez ushered me into the hall that led to the rest of the house, directing me into the dining room. One of the chairs had been pushed back from the table, but the hutch with heirloom dishes and the drawers under the sideboard were untouched. The hardwood floor gleamed as if newly varnished. One wall had framed family photos and another had pictures of churches.

We went through the swinging door into the kitchen, Deputy Mendez again maneuvering so that I went through first. I stopped in shock. The floor was covered with crumbs, globs of food, plastic lids, silverware, plates, boxes, and cans. The table was piled with open bowls. Some were empty, scraped to the last bite, and others were full, the food spoiling. The counters had spills left to harden, loaves of bread open with slices spilling out, soft-spread butter soupy at room temperature, and potato chips scattered from the end of a ripped bag. The refrigerator door was ajar due to a bag of oranges sticking out the bottom.

Across the hallway the other two bedrooms were immaculate, bedspreads wrinkle-free, pillows perfectly positioned as in a hotel, bureau drawers uniformly closed tightly, carpeting fresh.

The office was a large room with ample space for Uncle Bart's desk, books, and files, as well as for Aunt Betty's music and instruments. The desktop and all shelves, file drawers, and music cabinets were empty. Books, files, papers, and music were knee-deep on the floor, covering the carpet completely, making even one step into the room impossible. The phone was half-buried under the papers.

Speechless, I looked at Deputy Mendez. I couldn't read his expression, not knowing if he considered me a suspect or a victim.

He said, "The rest of the house is untouched except the back door was wide open. Can you tell if anything has been stolen? I don't want you moving anything, but does anything appear to be gone that you remember being here?"

I visualized the office. "I don't see the computer or digital piano. The last Christmas I was here Aunt Betty got Uncle Bart a top-of-the-line Macintosh. I suggested a laptop, but he prefers a Mac Pro desktop with a giant flat screen monitor. He got her the best digital piano made. I helped them get set up, on line, and connected. She can print out music by playing the digital piano. For years she did it all by hand. I've used her music with my church choirs in Greenwood City."

"She's had it published?"

"Oh, yes. She's well known in church music circles. Not all of what she writes is suitable for my choirs, since it's Mormon-themed, but most of it can be used in any church."

"Do you know how much the computer and piano are worth?"

"Digital piano."

"You mean keyboard?"

"It's electronic, like a keyboard, but it is larger and sits on a stand, so it looks like a small piano. It has full-sized keys and the feel and sound of a grand piano. It's a concert-quality instrument."

"You're making it sound expensive."

"The computer cost over $5,000 because of all the custom features Uncle Bart had put in. Add to that the best laser printer money can buy. The digital piano retailed for over $3,000. If all their software is gone—and music-writing programs are expensive—we're talking about a loss of over $10,000."

Officer Mendez stared at me. "We'd better check thoroughly to make sure the Ellsworths didn't move them to another room."

We started in the end of the house we hadn't checked, quickly going through the laundry room, bathrooms, and the closet containing the water heater and electrical box. We opened closets in all the bedrooms and even checked under the beds. A large wardrobe in the master bedroom was empty. We found nooks and crannies and concealed storage places I never suspected, but none contained electronic equipment.

Last we checked the family room. Here the storage spaces were plentiful, but filled with board games and puzzles.

As we emerged into the hot night air, I mentioned the tool shed attached to the carport. It was unlocked and contained all the chemicals and equipment for the pool, as well as shovels, rakes, hoes, an iron posthole digger, and a riding lawn mower.

Mendez radioed his partner. "Are you still following the track?"

"I lost it about five minutes ago. I haven't been able to locate it again."

Mendez contacted dispatch and said, "Page out the on call detective."

We stood by, perspiring and awaiting the detective. I told him my theory about the missing dogs. Deputy Weber returned from his unsuccessful search.

A plain white sedan arrived and a short Hispanic woman emerged. She was dressed in casual clothes, not a uniform. Her black hair was mussed and her eyes were puffy. The officers talked to her and then introduced her to me as Detective Sandino.

As I extended my hand to shake hers, Mendez intercepted my wrist violently, bent my arm behind my back, and had me handcuffed before I even thought of resisting. I stood there in shock as he read me my rights.

Chapter five

I sat in the back seat of the patrol car, hardly able to believe I was under arrest. True, Deputy Mendez said I was only being detained while they investigated further, but the handcuffs behind my back and the lack of a door handle said I was about to be jailed. The three officers were inside the house.

The patrol car motor idled, the emergency lights silently flashed, and the air conditioner cooled the cabin nicely. That comfort was more than offset by cramps spreading up my arms and into my shoulders. Mendez had been rough when he cuffed me, but he should have saved his aggression for criminals.

Although I hadn't felt comfortable around Deputy Mendez, I had been open and honest with him from the moment we met in Takamine's living room. I had discussed the problem of locating the Ellsworths. I had identified the missing electronic equipment. If I hadn't said what was missing, I had no doubt I wouldn't be in this predicament. For vandalism, wouldn't I be cited and released? How could he believe I was the suspect when I called the police for help?

The other officers were no better. They had stood by and allowed Mendez to manhandle me. Neither had showed any surprise when he had cuffed me, although Detective Sandino's eyes had flashed and her mouth had twisted for a second. I had the impression she didn't like what he did, but she backed him up without question.

I wished I had never agreed to house sit for the summer. If only I were getting married instead. That had been the plan until Janet found someone else. Just like that, our engagement was over.

After what seemed like forever the two uniformed deputies emerged from the house. Weber went straight to his patrol car and drove away. Mendez opened the door beside me and growled, "Step out. You're free to go."

It took a moment for his words to register. Finally Mendez assisted me to my feet and yanked off the cuffs. "Detective Sandino wants you inside."

I looked at him for a moment, waiting for an apology which didn't come. I watched him stow his cuffs on his utility belt neatly, then I went inside.

I found Detective Sandino in the kitchen. She was wearing latex gloves and bagging a cigarette butt. She smiled ironically and said, "Welcome to Ajo. I finally convinced Deputy Mendez you are legit."

"What made him think I was behind all this?" I waved my hand at the jumble of spoiling food.

"Oh, he didn't, really. He just goes by the book. You were being detained 'pending further investigation.' I wouldn't have cuffed you, but then Betty told me you were coming."

"What convinced Deputy Mendez?"

"This cigarette butt, for one thing." She held up the

plastic bag. "It's obvious you're no smoker."

"Really?" I hadn't considered the matter.

"Also, I found the tread of a tennis shoe that is quite a bit larger than yours."

"Thank heaven for small feet," I joked.

"The clincher was that note." She waved her hand at the refrigerator.

I walked over and studied the yellow paper which began, "Dear Ted…" It gave a watering schedule and instructions on caring for the pool.

"Thanks for going to bat for me," I said, rubbing my wrists and flexing my shoulders, still trying to work out the cramps.

"I don't 'go to bat' for suspects," said Detective Sandino sharply. "I strive to learn the truth."

"I'm all for the truth," I said, a bit giddy from my close shave with jail.

"Do you still have the note that was on the front door?"

"Note?" I shook my head. "I never saw one."

"I found fresh transparent tape with fragments of yellow paper on the front door. On the outside. As you can see, Betty loves to post notes."

She seemed to accept my statement without question, but I had just learned not to take appearances as truth. We moved to the office.

The detective moved books and files, stacking them to one side to allow her entry. I watched from the doorway, impressed with her graceful movements and with the curves that showed when her loose clothing pulled tight. She pointed out traces of dust on the shelves, but the desk where the computer had stood was clean.

"What does that tell you?" I asked.

"Never known a burglar to dust underneath something he stole."

"Are you saying my aunt and uncle took a computer, printer, and digital piano with them to camp in a national forest?" I asked.

Detective Sandino shrugged. She found more fingerprints on the back door. Continuing out back, she located footprints among the summer squash. She photographed them from various angles. There were wide spaces between the tracks which led under an orange tree. She reached up and plucked a black ball cap from the branches.

She muttered, "Rodney Zamecki." Showing the cap to Officer Mendez, she said, "Rodney Zamecki has been here. If we find him he might tell us who else is involved. This is not a place he would rob."

His eyebrows arched. "Why not?"

"The couple who live here are Mormons. Zamecki only wants alcohol and cigarettes."

"And food," I thought.

Mendez nodded. He drove away talking on his radio. Detective Sandino, humming as she worked, took digital photos, bagged evidence and dusted for fingerprints. Bored and tired, I wandered back to the bench under the chinaberry. I didn't want to be in Ajo a moment longer. Not only was it hotter than I had expected, the townspeople obviously didn't trust me. The two high school students I had met seemed okay, but I had no doubt that the general attitude toward me was more accurately portrayed by the cuffs and detention. Detective Sandino seemed a lot more friendly with Deputy Mendez out of sight.

I was half-dozing when I heard a rustle behind me.

Detective Sandino, illuminated by the moon, said, "I'm done here. If you'd like to clean up or move stuff around, feel free. If you find that anything else is missing, please call the sheriff's department and let me know." She handed me a card with the phone number and case number written on the back. She yawned.

"Why do you do it?" I asked.

"Do what?" But her impish face told me she knew what I was asking.

"Law enforcement. Come here at two in the morning." I was really asking why she was so committed.

She shrugged, yawning again. "Why do you give music lessons after school? Why do you do stage bands and parades and halftime shows and pep bands? Why do you direct choirs and cantatas and concerts? " She laughed at the surprise on my face. "Betty has bent my ear about you for years."

We discussed Aunt Betty and Uncle Bart for a moment before I asked for her advice on finding them. I mentioned their cell phones being "not available or not in the service area."

She wrinkled her brow, concentrating. "Have you considered talking to their children?"

"No. My main concern has been finding Betty and Bart, and getting into the house. Now that the door is unlocked, perhaps I can find their phone numbers in the mess in the office." They had five children. We had met at a number of family reunions and corresponded sporadically. "I did have a thought that Bart and Betty might have taken the dogs to the vet, but I wasn't able to confirm it."

"They also have voice mail on their home phone. If we can get the access number perhaps a message left for them could yield a clue."

"In other words, clean up the office and watch for these numbers."

Detective Sandino nodded, producing her cell phone. She punched a text message. "Maybe a text message will get through where voice can't."

"So you know my aunt and uncle pretty well."

She nodded.

"Does Uncle Bart often change plans on the spur of the moment?"

She put away her phone. "Some think of him as being impulsive, but there is always sound reasoning behind what he does. However, Betty would have found a way to get word to you. I'll bet she left that missing note on the door and told Gladys Takamine, not realizing she wouldn't be able to deliver the message. She might have left word with her children. They're very close."

"Thank you," I said. "You have given me hope and a plan."

"Also, when you're cleaning up the office, watch for paperwork on the computer, printer, and digital piano, especially invoices showing dates, prices, and serial numbers. Bishop Ellsworth is a meticulous record keeper." The diminutive detective started toward her car.

I followed, saying, "I take it you are well acquainted with the suspect."

"Rodney Zamecki. Let's just say he is well known in the department."

"How will I recognize him?"

"Hopefully we'll get him before you have to. But if not, he's big, probably 6'5", 250 pounds, blonde, blue-eyed. He always wears black. He is dirty most of the time. And he's strong. But as big and strong as he is, he had to have help, so be suspicious of everyone."

Perhaps it was the hour or my droopy state, but I wondered why he needed help. Detective Sandino picked up on it. "How big is that digital piano? Can you see anyone carrying it by themselves, let alone jumping a fence and getting away from the deputies?"

"I see your point," I said, feeling like a dunce. "To take the computer and monitor and printer and software in addition to the digital piano, I guess he would need a truck."

The detective nodded. "Getting a truck up here and carrying everything out would have woken the soundest sleeper. I'm assuming those things were already gone when you arrived. I'm still not discounting the possibility that the Ellsworths took them for some reason."

I doubted that, but I didn't say anything.

The detective added, "Also, it would be wise to have the house rekeyed. There was no forced entry. I wonder if the burglar has a key."

Detective Sandino opened her car door, and then hesitated. "By the way," she said, her friendly face catching the porch light so I could see every fleeting expression, "I'm glad you decided to call us instead of going after Zamecki yourself. I hate investigating homicides." Although her lips didn't move, a dimple suddenly appeared in her left cheek. Was she joking?

I lost no time going inside after the detective drove away. I had a tall glass of cold water from a cooler stand with bottled water. Having felt the heat of the local tap water, I knew why Betty and Bart had it. For the first time since the motel in Barstow, I wasn't hot. In fact, I was now wide awake and couldn't wait to tackle the office, even at two a.m.

In the office I went methodically, putting books on shelves first. Most of the books were scriptures and reference books for the Mormon religion.

Then I gathered the music and put it in no particular order into the music cabinets: choir selections and solos, hymn books, piano exercise books, piano lesson books, difficult classical pieces, popular music of all kinds, and the manuscripts of Betty's own compositions, many of them hand-written.

Putting them away made space to sit and inspect the contents of drawers that had been dumped. Nothing was ripped. There was no graffiti. I checked the contents of file folders against the labels as I put them in drawers. Sitting, however, was a mistake. I began to droop, pushing on until I awoke with a start, having lost about half an hour.

I got my suitcase out of the tent and went to bed in the guest room. I slept soundly the remainder of the night. I awoke just before dawn to get an early start on the office.

Making sure the door was unlocked so I could get back in, I strolled outside for a moment, scattering perhaps a dozen cottontail rabbits that had been munching on the lawn. The sun would soon rise over the royal blue mountains. Well above the horizon was a bright star that had to be Venus.

The temperature was finally halfway livable. The wind, which had died down while I sat waiting for Detective Sandino to finish her investigation, had not returned. Yesterday's dust storm was a distant memory. A mourning dove sang. A number of people were out walking for early morning exercise.

Turning around, I was arrested by the sight of the full

moon sitting balanced on the top of the ridge, a saguaro silhouetted in front of it.

I put the sprinkler on the lawn. The summer squash plants were doing fine. I studied the footprints for a moment, noticing something I had missed in the darkness. They were huge.

Chased inside when the sun blazed over the mountains, I went to the kitchen to get a bite to eat. I cleaned up the mess. Finding the milk hadn't spoiled, I ate some cereal. I checked my e-mail while I ate, glad the modem was still working. Nothing from my aunt and uncle. Nothing of interest. Actually, there had been nothing of interest in my email since my breakup with Janet. I returned to the office.

Next I found a phone book. Turning to the yellow pages, I picked the insurance company with the largest advertisement. Despite the early hour, I dialed.

The phone was answered by a gruff man, still at home, who nevertheless knew Bart Ellsworth and told me which company to call. Small town. I called.

This time I talked to a lady and reported the thefts. She said, "I just heard about that. Bart and Betty aren't back, then?"

"Not yet."

"Just give me the case number and I'll take care of everything."

I found she had expected the Ellsworths to leave later in the week.

I went back to the file folders. Among the legal documents was a property deed to the house next door. Bart Ellsworth had sold it to Shibasaburo and Gladys Takamine for the grand total of one dollar. One dollar?

I found information about the computer, laser printer,

digital piano, and a long list of software, including the music-writing programs. Dates, amounts, places, serial numbers.

I sorted through appliance warrantees, stock certificates, bonds, precious metal purchases, bank statements, bills—including the cell phone bill that confirmed I was using the correct number—tax returns, medical insurance, medical treatments, and finally, vehicles. A number of vehicles were on file, but all had been sold except the Lexus and a GMC pickup. Then there was a folder with page after page of neatly typed family trees.

I started on a stack of three-ring binders, each with a year marked on the spine, the journal of Bartholomew Ellsworth. It covered the last decade except for the current year. The first binder was hand written on lined paper with preprinted dates. The remainder were typed.

Among the miscellaneous items left on the floor was a small address book which had the phone numbers of all the Ellsworth children. I now had all the information I had been searching for except the access number for the voice mail, probably memorized and not written down.

I called the sheriff's station.

"Detective Sandino is on a call. May I take a message?"

I passed along the information on the stolen items, and the license numbers of the Lexus and GMC.

As I left the office, I looked back. The gaps left by the digital piano and computer were obvious.

I stepped outside into the heat to move the sprinkler, remembering Gladys Takamine. First I checked the pool chemicals, following the directions on Betty's note. I thought about vacuuming but didn't see any equipment in the shed that looked appropriate. Then I made the short walk to the Takamine residence. I wasn't happy about leaving the house unlocked. I would have to do something about that.

Again I enjoyed the rush of cool air as Takamine's door was opened, this time by a silver-haired man. He introduced himself as Cal Pinegar. I remembered he had cared for Shibasaburo yesterday. He said, "Good to meet you finally, Ted. Betty has extolled your virtues for years. Gladys is on her way home. The doctor diagnosed her problem as a TIA. I'm not sure what that is, but I gather that the attack is over."

"Oh," I said, remembering a friend of my parents in Wyoming. "A Transient Ischemic Attack. It's almost like a stroke, except the blood supply to the brain isn't totally cut off."

"Right," said Cal. "Something in the blood, like a clot or plaque, obstructs the blood flow through part of the brain. There are different symptoms depending on what part of the brain is affected and how much blood is blocked. Anyway, a friend is bringing Gladys home. She should be here in about an hour."

"Is her husband able to talk to me?"

Cal invited me in. Shibasaburo Takamine was seated in the living room. He was as tall as his wife was short. He had olive skin with darker age spots and thinning gray hair, combed straight back. The sides were in disarray. His most arresting features were his eyes. They were wild.

He looked at me, or rather his face turned to me, but his eyes were averted. He said something I couldn't understand.

"Hello, I'm Ted White."

"Shibasaburo Takamine," he said, drooling, his words so slurred that I wouldn't have understood if I hadn't known his name.

Cal said, "He understands what you say."

I told Shibasaburo about the missing Ellsworths. "Did they leave any word with you or your wife?"

Shibasaburo shook his head violently. "But," he said, "there was..." He quickly became unintelligible.

I tried hard to understand, but I failed. "I'm sorry. Could you repeat that?"

Shibasaburo tried, getting more and more excited, but to no avail. Finally he was reduced to one concept. "Blooarbee! Blooarbee!" As he became agitated, Cal stepped in to settle him. Shibasaburo lurched to his feet, but he had no control over them. He would have fallen if Cal hadn't grabbed him. He kept yelling, "Blooarbee! Blooarbee!"

Cal took Shibasaburo down the hall. Saddened that I was responsible for upsetting him, I waited until Cal returned.

I apologized. "Did you understand any of that?"

Cal shook his head.

"What happened to him?"

"It's a sad story," said Cal. "Not long after he retired he was involved in an automobile accident that left him brain damaged and partially paralyzed in his extremities. The driver of the other car was none other than his best friend, Bart Ellsworth. Since then, Bart has seen to it that the Takamines have what they need."

"How did the accident happen?"

"Shibasaburo had been to Phoenix and bought a new car. On the way back to Ajo he slowed down and turned left without adequately checking to make sure no one was passing. Bad driving habits are easy to fall into around here since normally traffic is so light. Unfortunately, a car was passing and Shibasaburo was struck broadside, rolling him down an embankment. Bart Ellsworth has lamented ever since that if he had recognized the car he would have known exactly where it was going to turn and he wouldn't have tried to pass."

I remembered the artwork next door. "He couldn't paint any longer. What a tragedy."

Cal nodded. "And he couldn't write or even type. He has a real communication problem. I think he sees and hears just fine, but he can't express himself the way he used to. Part of his frustration is that he knows how skilled he used to be, and he can't do it any longer."

Shibasaburo was trapped inside his own body. It gave me a new appreciation for being able to move and speak and sing.

Cal said that Gladys was another reason the town rallied around Shibasaburo. She was an excellent pianist and organist who willingly used her talents for several churches and for every music program put on in the town. The Takamines were part of the fabric of the community, and their tragedy had touched everyone.

When I returned to the Ellsworth home I heard the whistling before I saw the bicycle on the lawn. Marco Armendarez was gazing into the bed of my truck. The absurdity that I hadn't fully unloaded it despite the burglary suddenly hit me.

The black-haired boy looked up, removing his earbuds. "Morning, Mr. White. My dad sent me up to help you move in. Can I lend a hand?"

"Sure thing, Marco."

He grabbed a suitcase and clothes hanger while I picked up my musical instruments. As I opened the door for him, Marco said, "My dad wanted me to bring some other guys, but I told him you didn't have much stuff."

"I appreciate the help anyway."

On the way back for another load, Marco said, "That Lorenzo lied to me! He said there was a burglary here."

"Lorenzo who?" I asked.

"Carrillo. Why?"

"Did he say how he knew about the burglary?"

Marco's dark eyes widened. "You mean it's true? I don't see anything out of place."

"How did he know?"

"He heard it from Steve, but I don't know how Steve found out. So the Ellsworths are really missing?"

I drew a breath.

Marco cut in quickly, "Steve Paasch."

"I saw both of them yesterday," I said.

"In the pick-up pool, I'll bet," said Marco. "But the clerk already knew. I'm sure it's all over town."

"The insurance lady knew about it earlier, so I guess you're right." So much for easy answers.

"What can I do to help find the Ellsworths?" said Marco. "Do you think the burglar did something to them?"

"No, no. They weren't here when I arrived. The burglary didn't happen until the middle of the night. I'm sure there's no connection. Meanwhile, I need a lock-smith to secure the house while we try to find out where they are."

"T.J. Tatum."

The name rang a bell. "How do I get in touch with him?"

Finished unloading, we stood in the living room. "You can find him down on the main drag in that blue RV."

Something clicked in my mind. "Blue RV? Blooarbee? I wonder…."

The phone rang before I could call Tatum. Detective Sandino said, "Ted, I'm calling on my cell phone. How do you copy?"

"Fine," I said.

"We've located the Ellsworth's car." She paused. "It has been vandalized and there is no sign of your aunt or uncle."

Chapter six

Detective Sandino gave me directions to the Lexus, but I wasn't sure I could follow them. We exchanged cell phone numbers in case I got lost.

Marco Armendarez said, "I know exactly where it is. I'll be your guide."

"What about your parents?" I asked. "Won't they be worried?"

"Nah," said Marco.

"You've got to clear it with them. I can't take you otherwise."

"I'm sure my dad is in a meeting. You know school superintendents. I really want to help find the Ellsworths," said Marco. "I can guide you. Let's go."

"Your dad needs to know. He'll be supportive. He sent you to help me."

Marco struggled for something to say but came up empty.

Then I understood. His dad hadn't sent him, after all. I picked up the phone and handed it to Marco.

He reluctantly dialed, talked briefly to the secretary, and then took a deep breath. "Dad, remember I told you about Mr. Wh—"

Marco frowned, listening. "No, not yet. Yeah, I'll get it done, but listen, Dad, first Mr. White needs some help." He quickly outlined my problem and ended, "So he needs someone to guide him to Ellsworth Ranch."

Marco hung up and said, "I can go as long as I'm back to finish my chores before dinner."

Our destination was south of town on Bates Well Road. Marco guided me through town past the Plaza. He said, "This is a National Historic Site."

Remembering the Tucson, Cornelia, and Gila Bend Railroad sign on the ice cream parlor, I asked about Cornelia.

"Cornelia was the name given to the model town centered right here."

"Model town?" I prodded.

"John Greenway didn't like the dusty streets and wooden buildings with false fronts of typical boom-towns."

"If this was Cornelia, where was Ajo?"

"Over there between the three green hills." He waved toward the open pit.

The road passed through the gap between the white, powdery tailings dam and the higher, three-tiered, purple, yellow, and gray-striped rock pile.

Quite naturally Marco told me about his mother. She had been a physics professor at the University of California at Davis. He had idolized her and was striving to excel in science as she had. While I had never been on the UC Davis campus, I knew lots of graduates. Greenwood City was less than a hundred miles away. Marco and I had plenty in common from living in Northern California.

Before she died, Marco's mother and father had divorced. Marco had lived with her until the car accident that had claimed her life. He was not as close to his dad as he had been to his mom.

Marco said, "I really try to get along with my dad, but sometimes he does something that really burns me up."

By now we were on Darby Well Road turning onto Bates Well Road. I kept quiet, allowing him to share what he wanted, not pressuring him.

Marco settled more firmly against the seat of my truck and plunged in. "I had been in scouts for maybe a year. My dad didn't want me to join in the first place because the troop met at the LDS church, but it was the only troop in town. Mr. Ellsworth told my dad that they didn't teach religion in scouting, so he let me sign up. Then at a camporee up past Gila Bend this old windbag from someplace else broke that promise. He started out okay by talking about the Mormon Battalion trail that we were about to hike, but before he was done he was challenging the scouts to go on missions and to start now by preaching to nonmembers. In other words, to me. Not that anyone did. They acted kind of apologetic and didn't say much."

"I'm sorry," I said.

"Me, too, because I liked scouting, especially the campouts, and I knew my dad would yank me out as soon as he found out. But I guess Mr. Ellsworth heard what happened before we got back. He met us at the church and gave me a ride home. He told my dad what had happened and said how sorry he was about it. Boy was my dad mad. He ranted and raved until he got it out of his system. I've known him to complain for years about some things."

We passed a steel windmill that looked to be in good repair, but the blades were stationary. I said, "Is that windmill still in working order?"

"Sure. There's just no wind. The Ellsworth's windmill is all rusted."

"So their ranch isn't a working ranch?"

"No, not any more. The property is covered in arroyos. I wonder if whoever took the car got stuck in one."

"Arroyos?"

"A dry wash."

I must have still looked puzzled, because Marco tried again. "In most places, rivers and creeks always have water in them. Not here."

I nodded. "Thus the importance of wells. Darby Well Road. Bates Well Road."

"Ajo Well Road," added Marco.

I fell silent for a time, rattling over washboard. Before I was aware we were anywhere close to the ranch, Marco directed me to turn onto a pair of ruts. It was a good thing I had him along, because I would never have noticed them. We crept over a small hill driving on the edge of the wheel tracks to try to avoid high-centering my little truck. Beyond was a meandering line of small trees following the course of an arroyo.

We parked beside Detective Sandino's white sedan, a sheriff's department patrol car, and Border Patrol. We walked the last fifty feet to the sand.

From the edge of the arroyo the Lexus looked bad. All doors were open. The driver's side window was broken. The tires were buried to the axels in the sand.

We walked closer. Inside I saw smears and drops of blackish red on the steering wheel and dashboard. Blood.

A fair amount of it. The steering column was broken. The seats were covered with beer cans and wrappers. Wires dangled where there had been a radio. The glove compartment was open with papers spilling out.

Detective Sandino, dressed in a gray pants suit, came over with a uniformed officer. She said, "There are footprints heading north. We've got Border Patrol scouting around and several horses on the way to track."

"What about my aunt and uncle?" I asked, fearing the worst.

"They're definitely not here. That's all we know."

I was glad Detective Sandino was here. I liked the way she took time to talk with me, and I was glad she invited me to the crime scene. I didn't think many officers would have done that, certainly not Deputy Mendez.

The Border Patrol trackers arrived. One was a young guy who talked to Detective Sandino while his older partner unloaded two horses.

The Border Patrol agent who had been scouting returned and said, "It's a group of ten to twelve, and I'd say three or four are juveniles. There's a frequently used trail just over there. I'll bet that's where they were headed."

He left when the new guys mounted up and followed the tracks. Meanwhile Detective Sandino collected blood samples, fingerprints, and photographs.

Marco Armendarez had moved back toward the Lexus when my attention was on the Border Patrol agents and Detective Sandino. He was focused on the trash on the sand around the car: beer cans, cigarette butts, candy wrappers, string cheese packages, potato chip bags, beef jerky wrappers, and chewing tobacco cans. If the wind had been blowing today like it was yesterday, only the cans would have remained at the scene. I suddenly realized that I was thirsty.

Detective Sandino finished before the tow truck arrived. She approached me and suggested we sit on the bank. We watched Marco systematically studying the sand around the car. She stifled a yawn.

"Did you get any sleep at all?" I asked.

"Oh, several hours. I'll go weeks without being called out and then everything seems to hit at once."

"So who discovered the car?"

"Border Patrol. They came across it about the time I got to the burglary, but they didn't let us know until after five this morning."

As I gave her the update on Gladys Takamine, Marco called out, "I found something."

We hurried over to where he was kneeling. In front of him not two feet from the front passenger door, beside a drop of blood, was a wedding ring.

Chapter seven

Detective Sandino photographed the ring where it lay, and then examined it using rubber gloves. The gold band, dulled by a film of dust, was engraved inside with "March 14."

"It looks like Betty's," she said, "but whether she dropped it on the sand or in the car is impossible to say. Did the car get stuck first and then get vandalized? Or did the attack on the car cause it to get stuck?"

A flatbed tow truck arrived, backing into the arroyo. While we watched, Marco said, "Notice how the car came out this road, away from the ranch? I'll bet the car was stolen by UDA's. They broke the driver's side window and the steering column."

Detective Sandino nodded.

"UDAs?" I asked. "What's a UDA?" Gladys Takamine had mentioned the same term while looking through the Ajo Weekly Miner.

Marco shook his head at my ignorance. "An undocumented alien."

"We live in politically correct times," said Detective Sandino. "We no longer have illegal aliens or wets."

Marco continued, "Then the car got stuck. Notice how deep the sand is here."

I could see that the car didn't follow the tire tracks. Perhaps the broken steering column made it difficult to steer.

"I'll bet it was later trashed by kids," said Marco. "They're the ones who partied and left all the garbage. I've seen a lot of stuff left by UDA's, but never like this. Just empty water bottles and clothing."

"So you're suggesting," I said, "that the Ellsworth's parked their car out here to get it out of my way, and they went on vacation in their GMC pick-up."

Marco finished, "They just left before you got here."

This seemed plausible. After the tow truck headed toward Ajo, followed by the uniformed deputy, Detective Sandino said she wanted to check the ranch. Marco and I accompanied her. We left my truck and went in her unmarked car.

Our destination was over the rise and across the next valley. At the foot of a black mountain was an arroyo quite a bit larger than the one where the Lexus had gotten stuck.

As we got out, Detective Sandino handed me a canteen.

"Thank you," I said. "I was getting thirsty."

"It's difficult to stay hydrated in this climate," she said, lifting her own canteen. "Don't leave home without it." I followed suit and drank.

The ranch hardly deserved the name. An old windmill rusted peacefully away, its water pumping capabilities long forgotten. The tank was rusted with gaping holes in the sides. There was also a broken-down corral and a one-room shack with a sagging roof.

The ranch was situated at the entrance to a side canyon with rock walls seamed with cracks. Through the mouth of the canyon, I could see green trees and bushes in heavy shadows promising a lovely place to walk.

Marco and Sandino snooped around, but I was overcome by the heat and found a shady spot under a tree. I sat on the sand and drank deeply from the detective's canteen, remembering that in my youth I had written several adventure stories concerning "me and my canteen." My super-hero canteen would come to my rescue in improbable circumstances, belting the bad guys about to do me in or dousing the flames about to engulf me. Too bad this canteen couldn't locate my aunt and uncle and bring me word.

Detective Sandino came over and sat in the shade beside me. She had dark eyebrows, a dainty nose, and smiling lips. Her mouth naturally curved into a smile when her expression was neutral.

"Did you find anything?" I asked.

"Paw prints."

"I didn't notice any by the wreckage."

"Nor did I," said Sandino. "Fresh oil drippings show that a vehicle parked by the windmill, but the ground there is too hard and rocky for shoe prints."

Revived by the drink, I suggested we follow the path into the side canyon to check for evidence. From my seat on the sand I could see footprints and dog tracks on a well-worn trail. Marco came along and was soon ranging well ahead of us.

The path was shady. It ascended quickly as the canyon walls rose. This was no mere hill; it was a true mountain.

As we walked, Detective Sandino said, "Tell me why you expected to see your aunt and uncle. Couldn't they have gone camping, knowing you would get here as soon as you could?"

"They said they wouldn't leave until I came. Number one, I needed instruction on the pool. I still haven't figured out how to vacuum it. Number two, we wanted to visit. There was no rush for them. They were just going camping for the first three weeks. Then they planned to visit each of their children, making a grand family tour. Number three, they said the burglary rate has gone way up the last few summers, and they didn't want to risk leaving without a house sitter."

"So they disappear, and Zamecki breaks in," said Detective Sandino. "We haven't found him yet, but we will."

We were passing one of several spots where the creek-bed had standing water, slimy and green. The trees changed from mesquite to scrub oak as we climbed

I went on, "Aunt Betty invited me not long after Easter." I thought about my break-up with Janet. "I told her when I would leave and when I would arrive. We talked about playing Trivia and going to Organ Pipe. Betty wanted to show me her latest music. As it turned out, I was twenty-four hours late, due to car trouble. I called from Barstow when I realized I would be delayed, but no one answered."

"When did you last speak to either of them?"

"I talked to Betty on Sunday. Everything was all set."

In several places the canyon took big jumps in elevation, and we had to help each other up and over the giant boulders. Here a boulder had a large pool of water at its base where the action of the flowing water had scoured out a whirlpool. This pool was in perpetual shade and was so clear I could count every grain of sand in the bottom.

Detective Sandino looked closely at me. "Why you? Clearly the heat bothers you. They could have gotten someone local to house sit."

"What heat?" I said, grinning. Wiping my brow, my hand came away soaked. She waited while I squeezed between two boulders. "I had some setbacks in my personal life and needed to ponder whether to continue teaching. Should I sign my contract? Should I try to move to another school? House sitting on a hilltop, keeping cool in the house and swimming pool seemed like a good setting for getting answers. Plus, I looked forward to seeing my aunt and uncle. I like being in their home. I feel better, more settled, more at peace." I shrugged. "I can't explain it. I just needed to come."

"Why do you have doubts about continuing to teach?" Detective Sandino dropped her voice. "It's obvious that Marco sees you as the savior of the music program in Ajo. And he's pretty perceptive."

"The personal problems make it hard to stay in Greenwood City."

"Then come to Ajo," said Detective Sandino, as if that was the answer to all my problems.

I laughed. "Maybe I will, but I need to think things through and learn more about the situation here."

Reaching another jumble of boulders that seemed impenetrable, the detective and I discussed whether to turn back. Marco poked around. Suddenly I heard a voice from above my head.

"Mr. White, don't look up."

Of course, I looked up. Marco was standing on top of the boulders.

He said, "Why do people always look up when you tell them not to?"

"How'd you get up there?"

"Just go through the hole in the rock," he said. That reminded me of Shibasaburo Takamine's painting, and I wondered if this was the place he had brought his canvas.

Marco guided us to the passage. It looked like just another nook until you got inside and could see a small patch of blue up overhead. It took a contortionist's moves to get around the outcroppings and make it through. The lithe detective shimmied up easily. I got wedged when I was almost through and came to a stop. Looking up, I saw Detective Sandino peering down, her dark eyes probing to see if I needed help. She extended a hand to help me squeeze out of the hole, and I was amazed at her strength. I climbed into a tiny Garden of Eden.

This was indeed the place where the painting was made. It was also the end of the trail; the path ended in a box canyon. Water dripped from a hole in the rock, watering green grass and bushes beneath good-sized oak trees. The only difference that I could see from the painting was that there wasn't enough water to form a waterfall now, no matter how small. The magnificence of the location silenced us all. I found the exact spot where Shibasaburo sat to paint the scene. I rested for a moment.

There was no living soul in the canyon. No dogs. No sign of foul play. I imagined my aunt and uncle walking the dogs in the early morning. They would sit in this garden contemplating the beauties of nature, and then retrace their steps. They were still spry enough to make it through the hole in the rock.

Marco commented on the lack of water jugs and

other UDA debris, and I wondered if Uncle Bart packed out garbage every day.

There were some bird and deer tracks in the mud beneath the water drip, and another track with claw marks I was pretty sure was a bobcat. Buzzing insects, scuttling lizards, and calling birds made noise, but we were the only people around.

When she had finished searching, Detective Sandino came and sat lightly beside me.

I said, "Why did the band director resign?"

The detective glanced around. Finding Marco out of earshot, she said quietly, "Between you and me, he was afraid of kids. He was a good enough musician, but he didn't know the first thing about children. He didn't know how to make them mind. He would lock himself in his office during class. He had a doctorate in music, but he didn't know what to do with it."

"I've met a few like that," I said. "As soon as I locate the Ellsworths and verify they are all right, I'll make a visit to the school and see what I think."

"If need is a consideration, there is a definite need here," said Detective Sandino. "When the mine was operating, this was an affluent district that paid top dollar to attract and keep good teachers. Now salaries are about average, and our remote location hurts. But the students still have a right to a good education, and I think you would help that cause a great deal."

"How do you know—" I began. "Oh, you believe what Aunt Betty has said about me."

"Is there any reason I shouldn't?"

"Absolutely not," I said, laughing.

Detective Sandino looked up at the dripping hole in the rock. "When I was in school, the marching band was something that was cool. We took trips. We had an outstanding director, Mr. Schneider. The band helped school spirit more than anything else, and it affected how much we cared about all our classes and how much we studied."

"What instrument did you play?"

"Flute."

"When was the last time you played?" Many topnotch players nurtured their talent while in school, and then never touched the instrument again. They graduated, went into the work force, and no longer had opportunities to play. It was sad.

"At graduation." She smiled, her dimple appearing. "All the seniors who were in the band got to come down in caps and gowns to play our class song, 'Climb Every Mountain.' It was great."

When Detective Sandino was satisfied that there was no evidence to be found we retraced our steps and returned to the silent windmill. I was getting a little footsore and winded since it had been several months since I had been hiking, but the detective wasn't even breathing hard. We took a more direct path to the waiting car. Marco strayed further afield.

Just as we were opening the car doors, Marco called out. Reversing course, we ran to him. He was staring at spatters of dried blood beside a pair of tire tracks. Glass was scattered all around.

Chapter eight

"I tell you," said Marco, "that blood will turn out to belong to the UDA who stole the Lexus."

We were headed back to town in my truck. Detective Sandino had driven us out to my truck and then stayed to pursue the investigation.

"So," I said, "I gather you think UDAs are a big problem?"

"I don't know. I get my info about UDAs from a friend in Douglas."

"What does he think?"

"That we have it easy in Ajo. There have been murders in Cochise County, and he said it's only a matter of time before that happened. UDAs break in and steal stuff all the time. No one feels safe over there. People won't let their kids play outside if they're not with them."

"But I thought most of them are pretty mild-mannered," I said. "Aren't they just coming for work to send money back to their families in Mexico?"

Marco shook his head. "Things have changed. Now the drug cartels own the trails. You have to pay $2500 to cross. If you don't have it you have to carry drugs for the cartel."

"No wonder there have been murders."

"It's not near so bad here. The Lexus is the first car stolen by UDAs around here that I know of."

"So you don't think my aunt and uncle were attacked?'

"No."

Talk of drug cartels, home invasions, and murder did little to assuage my fears. What if the drug cartels were expanding into this area?

As we came into Ajo, I stopped behind the Red Ford Ranger pick-up pool at a red light. The boys I had seen before were seated in the water, but this time there were three girls with them. Loud music came from the pickup. The bearded Anglo teen yelled and shook his fist at me, but the music drowned out his words.

Marco said, "There's your entire percussion section."

"*My* percussion section?"

"Steve Paasch has the beard, Suzie Parker the sunburn, Lorenzo Carrillo the green cap, Gloria Mendoza the tattoo, Juan Rios the straight black hair, and Gabriella Lopez the blue suit."

"What are they upset about?"

Marco shifted uncomfortably. "I think they're blaming you for the disappearance of the Ellsworths."

"Why blame me?" I asked.

"Remember I told you I saw Lorenzo at Circle K this morning? According to him, Steve is saying that as soon as you came, the Ellsworths disappeared and you got their house; therefore, you must be the cause. I told Lorenzo that was stupid. He didn't like that. I think Steve's real reason for blaming you is to hide something he's done. That's what he does."

The truck turned when the light turned green. The sunburned girl, Suzie, cupped her hands and yelled an obscenity. The music drowned out her voice, but I could read her lips. Steve and Juan tried to splash my truck.

I drove straight ahead past the Plaza, and then turned toward the house, grateful to be out of sight of the angry teenagers. "What is Steve's connection with the Ellsworths?"

"Steve claims to be a pal of Mr. Ellsworth from when he was in Boy Scouts. Kinda sees him as the father he never had."

"No father? So it's just his mother?"

"Grandparents. He never knew his dad, and his mother is in jail."

As we passed the hillside with segmented cacti, I asked Marco what they were called.

He said, "Cholla."

I slapped my forehead, finding it still soaked from perspiration. "I should have remembered that."

Marco also identified the green-skinned, leafless trees as palo verde, the Arizona state tree. He said, "Ajo is really beautiful in the spring when the palo verdes are blooming. You can see bright yellow trees on every block. My dad is allergic to the pollen, though. He makes me do battle against them. I call 'em trash trees since they come up everywhere and I have to get rid of them."

We turned up the steep Ellsworth driveway. I said, "Do you think Steve and his friends will give you trouble since you defended me and now they have seen you riding with me?"

"Naw." Marco inserted his earbuds and rode off on his bike.

As I opened the front door I remembered I needed a locksmith. I checked the entire house before I dug up the phone number Marco gave me.

"T.J. Tatum," answered a rumbling voice.

"Hello, I'm Ted White. I need my house rekeyed. I wonder if and when you could do it."

"I'm not doing anything. How about now?"

"Great!" I gave him the address.

"That's the Ellsworth house, isn't it? I'm coming from Dorsey and Arizona 85."

"Are you in the snazzy blue RV?" Shibasaburo Takamine's voice reverberated in my mind, "Blooarbee, blooarbee."

"So you've seen it."

After completing the arrangements, I hung up. The doorbell rang. I said, "That was sure quick."

But the man at the door was Deputy Mendez. I felt my face harden. Deputy Mendez stood at attention until my usual manners surfaced, and I invited him in.

Sitting on the edge of the sofa in the living room, he said, "I've been briefed by Detective Sandino on the vandalism to the Lexus and on the associated blood at the Ellsworth Ranch. She directed that I start the missing persons case and do an official interview with you."

"Let's do it," I said. "Now, I do have a locksmith coming to rekey the house."

"Who is it?"

"T.J. Tatum."

"This shouldn't take long."

He was right. He was thorough, professional, and

brief. He didn't repeat questions trying to trip me up. He didn't bring anything to mind I hadn't already thought of, but at least law enforcement was getting involved.

I gave him the information I had gathered for Detective Sandino as well as the phone numbers of the Ellsworth children. I still hadn't had a chance to call them.

Deputy Mendez consulted his pocket notebook. "Do you know if Mrs. Takamine is back yet? I heard that her problem was a TIA."

"She should be. She was supposed to be here three or four hours ago."

"Let's go talk to her," said Mendez.

I was surprised he wanted my presence. I taped a quick note from Aunt Betty's yellow pad on the door for T.J. Tatum and accompanied Mendez next door.

Gladys Takamine was lying in bed looking tired but alert. "From what I've been told, I met both of you, yesterday. Forgive me for not remembering."

We introduced ourselves and stood on either side of the bed.

"Ted White," she said to me. "Betty talks about you all the time. I almost feel as if I know you. I'm sorry your wedding didn't happen."

"Me, too. One of those things." I didn't want to talk about it.

Gladys said, "I remember you came for a visit several years ago, but my husband had a battery of tests during that time and we were in Tucson. Bart pulled strings so that we get free medical care in return for testing various new treatments."

"I wondered why I hadn't met you."

"Betty told me you were going to house sit while they went on vacation."

"How are you doing?" I asked.

"The doctors have determined that one of my arteries is 75% blocked, and that's where the plaque broke off. I have to go back for more tests before they will clean it out. That's when they say I won't feel so good. Meanwhile, I have to keep quiet."

"Is that going to be a problem caring for your husband?"

"I've arranged for a home health nurse to come in mornings and evenings to help with the things I can't do yet. We'll be okay."

Deputy Mendez took up the questioning. "Did the Ellsworths leave word with you that they had changed plans? That they were going to leave before Mr. White arrived?"

"It would be like Betty to tell me, but I'm sorry, I don't remember. My last memory before waking up in the hospital is my husband calling me to tell me about a blue RV. I don't know if he had just seen it or if it was a distant memory."

"When did he tell you?" asked the deputy.

"I know it was early in the morning. Shibasaburo doesn't sleep all the way through the night. But I don't know which day."

"Where were they going on vacation?" asked Mendez. "We need to inform them of the burglary."

"Burglary!" exclaimed Gladys, struggling to sit up and then sinking back on her pillow. "What was taken?"

"The computer, printer, and digital piano," said Mendez.

"Betty will be heartsick," said Gladys. "Just heartsick. That setup has made her music writing so much easier. This is terrible."

"Where were they going?" repeated Mendez.

"Up in the White Mountains."

"Do they generally drive up in the Lexus or in the pick-up?"

"Heavens, Bart wouldn't go without his truck."

Mendez nodded with a small smile. "So they could well be on their camping trip." He thanked Gladys and got up, ready to leave.

I stood also. "The two paintings over at the house your husband did are tremendous. I saw the real hole in the rock today."

"That one he painted in person, but his portraits are done from photos. He has the ability to turn a wooden image into a living, breathing person with a life story."

Deputy Mendez waited at the bedroom door, his back turned to us.

I knew he wanted to leave, but I continued, "Is that what he did with my parents? That painting really touches me."

"It was such a little snapshot, you could hardly see it. I know he couldn't see their expressions. I asked him how he knew what to paint, and he said he studied the picture until he got a feel for it."

"Well, tell him he got it right," I said. "He got my mother's eyes perfect. I would have sworn my parents modeled for it."

"Well, I'll be," said Gladys, ignoring Mendez, who still stood with his back to us. I thought he was boorish. "We had that painting on the wall in the living room until just a few months ago, when he gave it to Bart and Betty as a thank you for all they've done for us."

I walked toward Mendez. "I'm grateful to have seen it. It's like my father is still alive."

As Officer Mendez and I returned to the Ellsworth residence, I asked how we would go about finding their usual camping place.

"I imagine their children know. I'll find out and have a forest ranger check on them. I'll be in touch. We'll find them."

Chapter nine

I pulled my note to T.J. Tatum off the door and began calling the Ellsworth children. George had a busy line. Scott had an answering machine. I left a message.

Colleen Draper, the oldest daughter, answered, but she wasn't even aware of her parents' vacation plans. "I've been out of the loop for a few months with a new baby. And living out here in Alaska...." She let the thought drift.

"I'm trying to find out if your parents told you where they might be. I was supposed to meet them at their home, but they're not here."

"No, they haven't said anything." She sounded vague and tired.

I gave her my cell phone number so that she could reach me any time.

Bob didn't answer.

Ellen Kramer, the youngest daughter, answered, saying that she had talked to her parents Sunday evening, but they hadn't called since.

"Did they say anything about a change of plans?" I asked. "They weren't here to meet me as we had planned.

They're missing."

"No. Mom talked about—Missing? What do you mean, missing?"

"They're not here. There's no message. No one knows where they are. I haven't found anyone who has seen them since Sunday."

"That's strange. Mom talked about taking you to the Ajo Historical Museum and down to Organ Pipe before they left. She also mentioned a tape of the local production of *Fiddler on the Roof* she wanted to show you. Where could they be?"

"On top of that, the house was burglarized last night."

"Oh, no! What was taken?"

"It appears to be the computer, printer, and digital piano."

"Not Mom's piano! That's her pride and joy. One of these years she's not going to go camping because she hates to be separated from it. And Dad spends a lot of time on his computer. Do you think there's a connection between my parents being missing and the burglary?"

I said, "I really don't know. But that's not all."

"Tell me." Her distress came through my cell phone clearly.

"Their Lexus has been found vandalized out near the ranch."

"What? And what do the police say?"

"A blue RV may have been seen here recently, but I don't have any specifics."

Ellen said, "I have a crazy thought. First, we need to find out if they are camping in their usual spot."

"Where is that?"

"In the White Mountains on the East Fork of the

Black River. They always stay in Buffalo Crossing campground and fish for trout."

"Where is that?"

"About twenty miles west of Alpine and ten or twelve miles south of Big Lake. It's remote. Nothing but dirt roads in that area. I'll call the ranger station in Alpine and see if they can find out if they're there. If they can't, I'll drive over and see. I'm in Payson, so I'm only four and a half or five hours away."

"Their cell phone isn't available or in the service area," I said.

"Cell phones don't work where they camp unless you go to Big Lake. There is a tiny area at the lake where you can get reception on good days, but that's the only place for miles and miles."

"What was your crazy thought?" I asked.

"That RV. Dad has pulled some crazy stunts over the years. I wonder if he bought it to surprise us and provide an extra bedroom when they visit each of us later in the summer."

"He didn't mention it?"

"No, but he might not."

"If he did buy it, surely someone local would know. So far no one has mentioned it, but I'll start asking." Gladys Takamine's brain might have lost that piece of the puzzle, too. We exchanged cell phone numbers and promised to keep in touch with any new information.

When I disconnected, the doorbell rang. A huge African-American man stood on the doorstep. "T.J. Tatum at your service," he said.

"I'm Ted White."

We shook hands. "You were recommended by Marco Armendarez."

"Nice boy," boomed Tatum, "but a bit troubled, eh?"

"I don't suppose you know the Ellsworths—" I began.

"Bart and Betty," interrupted Tatum. "I met them at church Sunday. Fine people."

"Oh, you're Mormon?" I couldn't hide my surprise. Another Mormon. Was Ajo like a town in Utah, or was I meeting so many Mormons because my relatives were members?

"Yes, I am," said Tatum, "but you're not."

"No. I used to supplement my teaching salary by directing church choirs. Mormons don't pay." That was another thing Janet Johnson had cost me. I had given up my choirs to spend more time with her, and I missed them.

Tatum chuckled. "We don't even have a paid clergy. But you didn't invite me here to talk. Let me at those locks." He rubbed his hands.

I hesitated. "You're probably wondering—"

"Not at all. Listen, this is a small town. I already know they stood you up and the house was broken into and the car was vandalized out in the desert. I know the thieves may have a key and that you are the responsible party. So let me at those locks. Time is a wastin'. The Ellsworths are my friends. We had lunch together on Sunday."

"You can start right here, then," I said, pointing at the front door. Tatum chuckled as he set down his tool box and laid out his tools. "Now about your lunch with my aunt and uncle?"

"Yes."

"Did they have any other guests?"

"Just li'l ole me."

"What time did you leave?"

"It must have been on towards four. I quite enjoyed their company."

"Did they make any reference to being gone later in the week or leaving earlier than they had planned? Anything you could read between the lines now that you know they left before I came?"

His hands stopped for a time while he considered. "Nothing comes to mind. Your aunt and uncle are skilled hosts. They got me talking about my favorite subject: myself. I didn't try to go against the flow and find out about them. I didn't see any luggage piled up waiting to be taken."

"Did you go in the office?"

"No." His hands had resumed their unerring work. "We spent the time in the living room and dining room."

"A blue RV was seen here recently," I said. "I gather it wasn't yours."

"No, once I park that monster, I leave it and putter around in my truck." Now that he was kneeling by the lock, I could see a small white truck parked beside my blue one. It seemed too small for such a large man.

"They didn't mention buying an RV of their own, did they?"

"Not even a hint."

I watched in silence, impressed at his speed. His hands seemed to know what to do without thought. "So how did you come to be a locksmith?"

Tatum looked at me while his hands continued working. "I was in construction, and locksmithing came in handy every now and then. I bought some basic tools, but mostly I figured out how to do it on my own. You might say I was born with a talent to tinker. After I sold the business and went on the road, it became a good skill to use to help people."

"What brought you to Ajo?"

"Arizona Highway 85. I'll bet you got here the same way."

It felt good to laugh. I hadn't done enough of that lately.

"Ah," he said, picking up his tools, "one down. Lead me to the next."

"That was sure fast."

"In construction, time is money. I may move more slowly these days, but work habits are hard to break."

On the second door, T.J. reminisced about missing persons he had come across in his travels. "Great Falls, Montana, with the wind screaming out of Canada. I found myself in a little laundromat trying to keep warm by the dryer. Another man was doing his laundry while his daughter played with a beat-up doll. He never looked at me. The girl was as charming as her dad was dour, except she gave all her attention to her doll. She fed and burped the doll with a heavy hand. She sang a lullaby, making up words as she went. She put it down for a nap. She even changed its imaginary diaper. It seemed odd that her father had brought her out on such a cold day. Was her mother ill or involved in a project? Had her mother died?

"My next stop was a grocery store. I picked up a milk carton with a picture of the same little girl, auburn hair, freckles, button nose, sweet smile. She was missing from another state, presumed to have been snatched by her father in a custody battle. I contacted police and they were able to restore the girl to her mother and two younger brothers. The man is still in prison, while last I knew the girl was a cheerleader in high school.

"It bothered me that I had no sympathy for the man, but in all the time I watched he never once spoke to his daughter or even gave her a smile. Why had he taken her? Just to spite his wife? I just can't figure out such hatred."

T.J. moved to the third door. "Portland, Oregon. A man had taken his mother shopping in a downtown department store. He always met his mother at the same time and place, but that day he never came. She reported him missing after waiting two hours. The police found that he had spent some time in a tavern, had one beer, and gone to meet his mother. Then he vanished.

"I happened to have business in the area and out of curiosity figured out his likely route. It involved taking an elevator. That elevator lurched and whined so badly that I was happy to get out and ready to go on a diet. Then I had a harrowing thought. I contacted authorities with my theory and they were able to check the elevator shaft. There he was at the bottom, crumpled and apparently dead. It had been two days. And then they saw a finger move.

"That man lifted himself up and called softly for help. He had been distracted while boarding the elevator. When the elevator lurched upward with the doors still open, he had tripped while trying to stop and fell into the shaft. He was able to make a full recovery. I felt really good about that one."

On the last door T.J. got to his real point. "Escondido, California. I was foreman on a new tract of homes, and I hired a good-looking gal to do the electrical. This was before I met my wife. I didn't need the help for several weeks, so I told her to start at 7:30 a.m. on June 30. June 30 came and went and she was a no-show. You get a lot of that in construction, so I was disappointed—did I mention that she was good-looking?—but not overly surprised. When she still didn't come the next day, I decided to check on her at home before I had to hire a replacement. No one was home. I checked with neighbors and found she had left the day before in plenty of time to get to the construction site, but she never came home that night. I reported her missing and got another electrician. A month later she showed up for work at 6:30 a.m."

"Oh," I said, "she got it backwards, 6:30 on 7/30 instead of 7:30 on 6/30."

"Yeah. She had gone to Vegas for a month, having gotten her notes mixed up. With a lot of missing persons, it's a simple communication problem involving time, date, or location."

T.J. picked up his tools, the job finished, and I had the new key.

"They could be victims of crime or accident," I said. "Where is their truck?"

"Or they could be camping, peaceably unaware of the mystery down here. It's a simple matter of miscommunication. Mark my word."

As he headed to the door, I asked, "How long have you been in Ajo?"

"Almost two weeks."

"How long will you stay?"

Tatum whistled a moment. "As long as I can help out and talk to nice folks like you."

"But why Ajo in the summer?" I asked. "If I were you, I'd put my shingle out in the Yukon, and come here in the winter."

"Ah," Tatum said with a twinkle in his eye, "you don't

practice what you preach. And had I done so, I wouldn't have met you."

I followed him out. "How much do I owe you?"

"You already paid it," Tatum said with a grin. "You listened to me jabber away. Anybody doesn't listen, I charge them double to make up for it. Most people don't even stay in the same room, and those that do don't really pay attention."

I held out a twenty. "Let me at least say thank you."

Tatum squeezed into his truck without taking the money and drove off with a cheerful wave.

I went back to the phone. I tried the Ellsworth children again, although it seemed silly to think of them as children when they were as old as, or older, than me. I got through to Scott this time.

"Hey, I talked to Ellen," said Scott. "And I'm not worried."

"Why not?" I asked.

"Dad plays mind games all the time. He calls them other things—logic, psychology, brain teasers, seeing through the camouflage—but they are mind games. You're the victim this time."

I couldn't think of anything to say.

"I don't fault him," Scott continued. "He helped me learn to be observant and to think. He helped shape me. I've been known to do the same with my children. It helps to keep us on our toes, our minds sharp and observant."

"That's easy to say," I said, "but what if it's not? The hypochondriac who always cries wolf can really have a heart attack."

"The classic dilemma. I won't spoil his game. The next move is yours. Oh, I almost forgot. Just to give you another wild goose to chase, I happen to know that my little brother is buying an RV. Ellen said one might have turned up at the house."

"Bob?" The youngest brother?

"He was trying to work out financing, but he makes big bucks as a world class chef. I doubt he has had any trouble coming up with a down payment."

"You think Bob bought an RV and unexpectedly came to Ajo, and that it was his blue RV that Shibasaburo Takamine saw?"

"Something like that."

"What would be his purpose?"

"To go on vacation with Mom and Dad."

I obtained the name of the restaurant Bob worked for in Denver.

After completing the call, I got the phone number for Bob's restaurant from information and called. No one would talk to me about their prize chef, however. "Call back tomorrow," was all I got.

Finding the names of Ellsworth friends and relations who lived outside Ajo in the address book, I continued making calls, but an hour later I had no new information. I had asked if the Ellsworths were known to be getting a new RV. No one had heard anything about it.

I checked my e-mail. Nothing.

Tired of sitting, I wandered around the yard. A thermometer in the shade near a ceramic frog registered 104°F, up nine degrees in one day. Still no wind, even in the later afternoon.

The pool floor still needed vacuuming. This time I looked for a vacuum switch. Commercials on TV showed snakes coming out of the walls to vacuum automatically. The switches and buttons weren't labeled, so I tried several. I turned on the filter (which was on my 'to do' list), but no vacuum came to life.

I saw the Native American with the sooty black clothing working next door. I called to him, but he ignored me, continuing his chores.

I called Gladys Takamine and asked if she knew anything about the operation of the pool.

"No," said Gladys, "but you know who is a whiz with machinery like that is Manny Molina. You may have noticed him doing yard work at McBain's on the other side of the Ellsworth's."

Deputy Mendez had mentioned him. "Does he work at that industrial plant mining the slag heap?"

"And gets black with slag dust. That's him. Such a waste. He works twenty-four hours a day."

"I can think of worse things to do."

"You don't understand," said Gladys. "He has such a musical gift, and it's going to waste. In high school he was the best trumpet player I have ever heard."

"I just saw him and tried to talk, but he ignored me. Does he have a problem with Anglos?"

"Manny? Heavens, no. He didn't hear you. He's deaf."

"How can he play the trumpet, then?"

"He was born with a congenital hearing defect in his right ear that was diagnosed when he was five-years-old. When he took up the trumpet in school, he was just a natural. He was already all-state when he was a freshman. By his senior year, he had a free ride to any college he wanted, he was that good. But he contracted Meniere's disease in his good ear and ended up having to have the acoustic nerve severed to stop the attacks. Believe it or not, he was still the best player in the school. He learned to adjust his embouchure to make the correct notes. He could feel with his lips and face how to make each note, and he could judge volume and blend with the band by looking at Charlie's face."

"So now Manny works at the slag plant and does yard work?"

"He started working for Aaron Jones at the nursery while still in high school. After graduation he went full time and now has the most business in town. He cares for the Plaza, the Art Gallery, several RV parks, and lots of homes, especially in the summer. He really has a magic touch with plants. He did my landscaping as well."

"Why didn't my aunt and uncle just hire him, then?" I asked.

"Betty said she wanted to give you a chance to get out of Greenwood City. She said you needed a change of scenery after the wedding was cancelled."

Before hanging up, I mentioned that I had had the locks rekeyed.

"I guess my key won't do any good, then," said Gladys.

"You had a key all this time?"

"Right here in my bedside table." I heard a drawer opening. "That's funny. It's gone! Well, no matter. It won't work now, anyway. Did you try the key Bart keeps hidden under the ceramic frog near the pool?"

She laughed at my sputtering into the phone. "Here I knew where two keys were. The knowledge was locked away in my brain, and you weren't able to get in." She paused. "I just can't picture Betty going off without getting word to you. She's the most organized person I've ever known. There had to be a note or some other means to get word to you besides my faulty brain."

"There was possibly a note on the front door, but it apparently blew away. Detective Sandino found the tape, but not the note."

"Well, that's a good sign. I've been worried sick by this."

"The detective is pretty sharp."

Gladys said, "Isn't she, though?"

"You know her?" I asked. Dumb question. Everybody knew everybody here.

"I should say so. I was her babysitter for a number of years. She was smart as a whip. I remember learning to play chess together. I was tickled pink to see her get involved in band and choir when she got older."

"Choir?" I asked.

"Oh, yes, she's a choir director and an absolute natural at it."

It would be fun to sing in her choir, I thought, as I returned the cell phone to my pocket. I went straight to the ceramic frog. It was heavier than I expected. I actually grunted while picking it up. There was nothing there. The key was gone.

Chapter ten

I checked all around the ceramic frog and couldn't find the key anywhere. With no sign of Manny Molina at the McBain residence, I went inside to the blessed cool.

I sat pondering in the comfortable living room. Not only did the mystery of my aunt's and uncle's where-abouts plague me, I couldn't believe the suffering I encountered in this small town. Manny Molina, a young man with tremendous musical talent, struck deaf. Shibasaburo Takamine, a talented painter, crippled soon after retirement. Steve Paasch, an at-risk young man, never knowing his father and whose mother was in jail. Marco Armendarez, an intelligent young man, whose mother had died young.

In Greenwood City I didn't know anyone who had faced challenges like this, and I knew why. I didn't get close enough to people to learn their private heartaches. I knew a lot of people on the surface, but there was always a distance, a barrier I was comfortable with.

Here, because the Ellsworths were missing, I had been forced to break through the barrier. If they had been home, I would have enjoyed a visit, but I would have missed getting to know Detective Sandino, Gladys Takamine, T.J. Tatum, and Marco Armendarez.

I was impressed with Marco. His mother's death drove him to follow in her footsteps in science. Despite his differences with his father he wasn't rebelling. He was a good kid. And he played the trombone!

The doorbell rang. Deputy Mendez was back.

He swelled, looking down his nose at me, no mean feat since I was taller. He said, "Will you stop meddling in my case? No matter who I talk to, you've already talked to them, and they don't want to talk to me. Back off and let me do my job."

I thought it was his attitude, not my meddling, that was causing him problems, but I said, "You're welcome to all the information I've gathered."

"I don't need your help. Just back off."

"I understand," I said.

"Good. I obtained the Ellsworth's usual camping location. Rangers out of Alpine will make a visit this evening. I'll advise when they locate your family." He turned on his heel and marched back to his patrol car. He drove off spitting gravel.

I got a drink of water and checked my watch. I was late for my dinner appointment with Detective Sandino at Pizza Paradise. We had arranged to meet to share information. Plus I was hungry. I hadn't eaten since having a bowl of Corn Chex at breakfast.

The restaurant was virtually empty when I arrived, and the detective wasn't there. I ordered a medium pizza, two salad bars, and a pitcher of root beer. I reveled in the air conditioning while I waited, watching the parking lot and walkway leading to the entrance.

Perhaps twenty minutes passed while I idly watched

cars come and go, thinking about the Ellsworths. The manpower of several law enforcement agencies was tackling the mystery, but nothing really seemed to be happening. All we knew for sure was that my aunt and uncle weren't where they planned to be. Everything else was conjecture.

Deputy Mendez, a pain to work with, was convinced they were camping. Detective Sandino, a joy to work with, could only painstakingly catalog evidence.

Anything could have happened. What if their truck had simply died in the desert? In this heat, how long would they last? What if the blood at the ranch was theirs? They would need medical attention. I should be canvassing hospitals—what was I doing sitting here in a podunk pizza place?

Detective Sandino, wearing a tan pantsuit, slid in opposite me just as the pizza was served.

"Good evening, Detective," I said, trying to shake my depression. She smiled, her dimple staying in place. I began to feel better.

"Since we're obviously going to work together on this case," she said, "perhaps I'd better re-introduce myself. My full name is Blanca Alicia Sandino, but everyone calls me Sandy. So my first name is the same as your last."

I smiled at that. "So you're willing to work with me, are you? I've just been told to back off by Deputy Mendez."

"Join the crowd. Mendez says that to everybody." We got up and went to the salad bar.

"But there's no one I would rather have backing me up. He's fast and fearless. He remembers everything there is to know about the bad guys. He's very effective dealing with them."

"So why did you sic him on me?"

Sandy laughed, a musical sound. "We were short-handed today."

"One thing that has impressed me about Ajo right off," I said, "is the number of musical people I've met. Gladys Takamine and Aunt Betty, of course. Marco plays the trombone."

"He's really good."

"You play the flute and direct. The girl at The Milky Whey is another flautist."

"Debbie Piccioli. She's better than I'll ever be."

"Piccioli? And can she play the piccolo?"

Sandy's laugh was a joy to hear.

"And then there's Manny Molina," I said. "Gladys thinks he can still play."

Sandy nodded. "But only if the right director comes along—someone willing to work with him and inspire him."

"Last night in the tent, I was so hot I couldn't stand it. I wished I were back in Northern California. Then the burglary, and there I was in handcuffs. It seemed like the whole town was against me. If I could have signed a contract to stay in Greenwood City at that moment, I would have done it." I stopped.

"And now?"

I was enjoying the air-conditioned restaurant and Sandy's dimpled smile. "Ajo definitely looks better when there's a refuge from the heat."

Sandy nodded in agreement, and then shifted into command mode. "Did you make any progress on the Ellsworths?"

"Gladys had a key to the house, but it's missing. She said there was one under the ceramic frog, but it's missing, too."

"I'll have to ask Rodney Zamecki how he acquired one."

"You've found him?"

"No," said Sandy, "but he never stays hidden very long."

"At least the house has been rekeyed."

"What'd you think of T.J.?"

"What a whiz on locks, and I enjoyed his stories, too. He thinks miscommunication is at the root of the problem."

"I talked with Deputy Mendez. He found some early morning walkers who saw the blue RV."

"When? Where? Why didn't he tell me?"

Sandy didn't laugh, but the dimple in her cheek was well defined. "The witness saw it two days ago on Scenic Loop about five-thirty in the morning. It was following the green Lexus. The witness saw Bart in the Lexus, but he didn't see Betty."

"Tuesday morning. That road goes to the ranch, too, doesn't it?"

"Yes."

"I guess the truck could have been parked out there already and they could have just switched vehicles."

Sandy nodded. "Or they could have gone in the RV. I gather you talked with several of your cousins. Mendez said they didn't want to tell him much."

I said, "I'll bet he was more blunt than that."

Sandy's laugh was as musical as before.

I continued, "Colleen didn't know anything. Distance, a new baby, and a busy schedule keep her out of the loop. Ellen said she would call the forest rangers to check her parent's usual camp site. She'll go check in person if they can't find them. She plans to come here if they're not camping. Scott thinks Uncle Bart is playing mind games on me. He didn't take their disappearance seriously at all."

Sandy's eyes gazed straight at me. "Don't be fooled by Scott. He'll be the first one on your doorstep."

"I'll keep trying to reach George and Bob, despite the warning from Deputy Mendez."

"Do it," said Sandy. "Border Patrol is still following the track of the UDAs. They are now north of Crater Range. I checked with U.S. Customs and there is no record of the GMC pickup crossing the border."

"Why would it cross?"

"That's where 90% of stolen vehicles are taken, around here."

"Of course," I said.

"I didn't call the rangers in Alpine because Mendez said they gave him a hard time, which ticked him off. They had already talked to Ellen. All he got was that they planned to check either in person or by ham radio, but the camp host doesn't start his generator and check in until eight p.m. Also, I worked through the telephone company and got their voicemail, but there was nothing useful for our purposes among the messages. You recorded well," she added with an impish grin.

Done eating, we continued talking, sipping root beer.

I said, "So what do you think of T.J.'s conclusion that miscommunication is the key?"

Sandy set down her soda. "I tend to agree with him. I've seen nothing that really waves a red flag that something bad has happened."

"But what about the burglary? What about the vandalism? What about the blood? It seems to me that there are red flags everywhere."

Sandy kept cool. "Vandalism, yes. Burglary? That remains to be seen."

"But—"

"Yes, three valuable items aren't there, but were they stolen? And the vandalism in the house wasn't serious. There was no graffiti, no spray paint, no gang symbols, no satanic signs, and no excrement. I've seen much worse."

"What about the attack on the car?"

"The evidence points to more of a party atmosphere."

"There was blood."

"But whose?" asked Sandy. "We can't definitely say your aunt and uncle were in the Lexus when it was trashed."

"The wedding ring," I pointed out.

"It could have been dropped in the car and kicked out later."

"*Could* have been, and my aunt could have been wearing it when she was brutally attacked. You see, you're making every excuse not to push the investigation."

Sandy looked me in the eye. "But the investigation *is* being pushed. Things *are* happening."

"I don't see it," I said, trying to stare her down. She didn't flinch. "You haven't even found the prime suspect."

"He'll turn up."

"You see," I said. "'He'll turn up.' That's your whole attitude. You're letting things happen at their own pace. You're not forcing the issue and really searching for him. My aunt and uncle could be in great danger, maybe stranded out in the desert or bleeding to death, and you say, 'Oh, he'll turn up.'"

Sandy sighed, but still looked me in the eye. "The whole department is working on this. It's our number one priority, and overtime is mandated to further the investigation."

"Convince me," I said. "How do you know they're not bleeding to death out in the desert or stranded without water?"

"Border Patrol is all over the place on the ground looking for them. They have twenty times the personnel the sheriff's department has. They have sent their Blackhawk helicopter to check from the air. They haven't seen anything yet, but they will start again at first light."

"What if someone got them to a hospital already?"

"We have all hospitals and medical centers in the state on alert, but so far nothing."

"What about the GMC? Did you check anywhere besides the border?"

"We sent out a statewide alert on the GMC pickup, thanks to your information. We have entered Elizabeth 'Betty' Ellsworth and Bartholomew 'Bart' Ellsworth in the computer data base as 'missing persons, endangered.'"

I took a deep breath to ask another question, but my mind was blank. I let out my air. "You have convinced me," I said. "I don't know what else you can do. I apologize for my behavior."

Sandy's cell phone rang, cutting me off. She punched a button and said, "Hello, Detective Sandino."

She listened and then said, "Good. Where did you find him?" Her eyes smiled at me as she listened. She turned off the phone and said, "I've got to go back to the sheriff's station. Rodney Zamecki is in custody. Deputy Mendez, off duty, arrested him."

Chapter eleven

Driving back to the Ellsworth residence, I reflected on the meeting with Sandy. I found it easy to talk to her. When I first met Janet Johnson I was so tong-tied I had difficulty saying anything, much less carrying on a conversation. It had taken weeks for brain freeze at the sight of her to begin to thaw. With Sandy I had been comfortable from the start.

I wondered if the difference was the situation. Asking Janet out had meant that I was interested in her. Meeting with Sandy was in an official capacity investigating burglary, vandalism, and missing persons cases, yet our conversations were far different than typical law enforcement interviews, such as those with Deputy Mendez.

I was sure of one thing, however. I did not want a dating relationship so soon after being summarily dumped by my former fiancée. I had fallen like a ton of bricks for Janet and still hurt from the break-up. No matter what attraction I might feel for Sandy, I had to keep this relationship on a professional level. Nothing personal.

Besides, Sandy was a detective. She was a trained

professional at eliciting information. Her manner toward me was only a means to further her investigation.

While approaching the Ellsworth residence, I thought I saw movement near the house, a fleeting thing that might have been imagined. I parked the car and checked around the exterior. Nothing was out of the ordinary. The doors were secure.

I went in and continued calling my cousins. This time I got through to George. He, too, had no idea what had happened to his parents. He had been teaching summer school all day, so Ellen hadn't been able to break the news.

"Man, that's worrisome," he said. "It's not like my parents not to tell anyone what they're doing."

"My thoughts exactly."

"Growing up we were taught to leave word where we were going. My parents could say with certainty where each of us was, and we always knew where they were. It was automatic."

"Especially since they knew I was coming."

George said, "Is it possible that they thought they left you word and you didn't get it?"

I admitted it was very possible. I explained about my cell phone being left accidentally turned off, the missing note, and Gladys Takamine's TIA.

"You know," said George, "my father has really gotten into family history lately. I wonder if he got a lead and couldn't wait to track it down."

"Is your dad really that impetuous? I know your sister Ellen thinks so, but…."

"Dad is not impetuous," said George. "Everything he does is well thought out, but his mind works so fast he can see all the implications before the rest of us."

I digested that. "Can you give me an example?"

"Okay. Every year we went fishing at Buffalo Crossing. One year we loaded up and started north as usual. On the way to Gila Bend, Dad said, 'I hear the water in the Black River is low this year.'"

"Why does the water level matter?"

"Low water heats up too much for trout, and Game and Fish won't stock. If they don't stock weekly there, fishing is terrible."

"So what did you do?"

"We went lake fishing on the Mogollon Rim near Heber. We cared about the fishing, but dad had other things in mind."

"Like what?"

"That year gasoline had gone up a dollar a gallon, and where we went was half the distance to Buffalo Crossing. In addition, his sister who lives in Heber had just had surgery. We were able to visit her daily to help out, whereas we would have stopped by only twice if we had gone to the usual place."

"So," I said, "you think it's possible that your dad suddenly learned something or had an opportunity that couldn't wait a day or two until I came. I'm still not seeing it. How could it be something to do with family history? What could the rush be? Family history records don't just disappear. He would still have waited a few days."

"I can think of some ways family history records could be in jeopardy, but let's suppose you're correct. Could the records be an excuse? Could the real reason he left suddenly be that he needs to be somewhere else?"

A thought struck me. "Or just away from here?"

"It could be anything," said George. "Especially an

opportunity to be of service."

"What about the RV? A big blue RV was seen in the area Tuesday morning early. It followed your parents out Scenic Loop. Ellen thinks Uncle Bart possibly bought it for their summer tour visiting all their children. Scott thinks Bob bought it to go camping with your parents. I'm wondering if it has a connection with their sudden disappearance. Do you have any thoughts on it?"

"I think we can eliminate Ellen's thought. Dad can't stand RVs. He'd have gotten one years ago otherwise. He and Mom like to rough it. They've always tent camped, although in recent years they have 'gone soft,' in Dad's words, by sleeping on an air mattress."

"What about Bob?"

"I haven't talked to him lately. He's moving into a new house and hasn't had time for more than 'hi' and 'bye.' But why is it important to find out whose RV it is?"

"It's just more information that will help us figure out what happened and where your mom and dad are."

"Man, I wish I could come down to help out, but I'm teaching summer school. I signed a contract stipulating that I couldn't miss any days. There is no provision for substitutes. I'm required to be here. Man, I'm sorely tempted to come anyway."

"I'm a teacher, too," I said. "Our summer school contracts require the same commitment."

"What I can do is review all the e-mails Dad has sent over the last few months. Maybe he said something about family history or something else that will provide a lead. Maybe he has consulted with a professional genealogist. I know he was having problems."

"Good idea," I said.

"Hardly a week goes by without something from him. Except this week, come to think of it."

When I hung up I checked my e-mail, again. Since there was still no reply, I sent off another e-mail to Uncle Bart, just in case.

I prowled restlessly around the house, feeling frustrated. The house seemed stuffy. When I loosened my collar, my neck was wet with perspiration. I held my hand up to a vent. The air was lukewarm. Something was wrong with the cooler.

I grabbed my flashlight and went outside, where the air was decidedly more pleasant than inside, although not cool by any means. The cooler was difficult to locate in the dark. My flashlight disturbed a large slimy toad, which moved with surprising speed, considering it was built like a tank. Also, its presence disturbed me. Colorado River toads are toxic to dogs. Could one or both of the dogs have gotten poisoned? I had forgotten to track down the veterinarian, but surely if the Ellsworths had taken their dogs to the vet in Phoenix, they would have made contact with me by now.

The bats swooped down and drank from the pool. The coyotes howled in full chorus not far away. For a desert, this place was alive with creatures.

I went all the way around the house, shining the flashlight behind every bush, before I thought to look on the roof. There was the cooler. I had thoughts of sleeping outside, again, rather than climbing an unfamiliar roof in the dark, but the break-in the night before stopped me from seriously considering it. Plus the moon was rising, offering hope of illumination.

Then I heard a laugh, quickly stifled, a sound familiar to a school teacher. There were some kids somewhere nearby. It was likely that the cooler problem was vandalism.

Should I call the sheriff's department, yet again? My instincts were against it. I could just hear my students (if I got the job here): "That Mr. White can't do anything on his own. He has to call the police for everything."

I imagined Deputy Mendez asking what was wrong. "The cooler isn't cooling."

"Why is that vandalism?"

"Because I heard a stifled laugh."

"Did you see anyone doing the damage?"

"Well, no."

"Couldn't the cooler have just had a mechanical breakdown?"

"I suppose so."

"Where are the suspects?"

"Out there in the darkness."

"Give me a description."

"Get them to laugh, and I'll know who did it."

I had better fix the cooler and be done with it.

Since my flashlight wasn't powerful enough, I went to the tool room by the carport. I had noticed a two-foot long mag light earlier. I had switched it on briefly in the shed to make sure the batteries were good, and it lit up the small room like the sun.

In the darkness, I approached the west wall. The rising moon cast deep shadow on that side. I listened for several minutes. I could hear small movements, a whisper, an aborted giggle. Suddenly I turned on the mag light, aiming it in the direction of the sounds. They were coming from under a large palo verde tree, stark yellow green against the black background. The tree shook wildly as if a herd of javelinas was trying to escape, but I couldn't see anyone or anything.

I heard something slamming into a brittle bush, branches snapping like gunshots. There were muffled oaths. I ran toward the carport, still aiming the light, trying to get beyond the huge tree to see who had emerged. They were gone.

I switched off the light, letting my eyes adjust to the darkness. I saw nothing more. The rising moon illuminated the mountain beyond the deep arroyo, but the foreground was black.

Finding a ladder and tool box, I climbed to the roof. The tile roof was steep, and although it wasn't slippery, I had to master the knack of walking on it without falling. I opened a side panel, suddenly noticing a bright amber light in the sky beyond the cooler. I stood there holding the panel while three more amber lights winked on. Only my high vantage point allowed me to see them. They would have been behind the citrus trees if I was down in the yard.

The amber lights made no sound. I thought they were quite a distance away, perhaps as far as Crater Range, drifting slowly downward. The first one suddenly winked out.

Then I noticed sparkling white lights among the steady background of stars. Some brighter than others, the lights seemed to bounce around the heavens—the blinking running lights of planes. I counted five before I stopped looking. The sky tonight was alive.

Turning my attention to the task at hand, I found I was still holding the side panel. I set it on the roof and it started sliding. I grabbed it, but disturbed my own perch. I slipped, barely managing to hook my elbow on the cooler.

Leaning the panel on the uphill side of the cooler, I looked inside. I held on to steady myself. The water wasn't reaching the pads and could not be evaporated to cool the air. The water pump was pumping, water was in the vertical plastic tube, but no water was dripping on the pads.

I climbed down and shut off the cooler. The controls were in the house. I paused by the wall in the shadow of a tree, listening to see if anyone had returned. I heard nothing. Back on the roof, I discovered a wad of wood shavings clogging the center so that no water could get to the spider-like tubes that distributed the water. I cleaned it out, reconnected the plastic tube, and turned on the cooler again. When I climbed back up, water dripped onto the pads.

Balancing precariously, holding the flashlight under my armpit, I lifted the side panel to put it back in place. At that moment I heard the whizzing of an approaching rock. I dropped the panel and threw myself to the roof on my back. The rock flew by, missing me by inches.

Suddenly I realized I was sliding. I was already beyond reach of the cooler. My flashlight preceded me over the edge of the roof, the light descending in an arc. The panel hit the ladder, tipping it over so that both fell together with a clatter, angling to my right. Meanwhile, I was sliding more slowly due to the friction of my clothing against the tiles, but I couldn't stop myself. I tried to dig in my heels to halt my slide, but they slipped off as if the surface was oiled. This seemed to propel me faster. My feet slithered off the edge of the roof. I was going down.

Chapter twelve

In desperation I heaved myself over on my stomach, trying to hang on the edge and grab something with my hands. There was nothing to hold. I slowed, but I couldn't stay on the roof. I dropped to the grass in slow motion, landing on my feet facing the house, then going down on my side away from the ladder.

I lay on my side on the lawn, gratefully inhaling and exhaling. If the rock thrower had wanted, he could have walked right up to me. No one came.

I felt shaken up, as if my bones had come apart and snapped back in place slightly out of alignment, but I was able to sit up and then to stand. No bones were broken. I retrieved the panel from the lawn, finding a few scratches and one corner bent out of shape. I took it to the tool shed and pounded it straight with a hammer.

Then I had to force myself to stand the ladder back up and take the panel back to the cooler. I hated the idea of going back up, but the need for cool air persuaded me.

This time, I was successful. The panel fit in the slot with a little wiggling. I was soon safely back on ground.

I checked the interior of the house before putting the

ladder away. Cool air again circulated.

Too keyed up and sore to sleep after falling from the roof I went to the office, the coolest room in the house. My eyes lighted on the diaries. Selecting the first volume, I turned to March 14 and confirmed Bart's and Betty's wedding date. That as good as verified that the ring found on the sand by the Lexus was Betty's.

I flipped through a number of volumes, stopping to read here and there, getting a feel for Uncle Bart. Much of it was mundane, but startling observations kept leaping out at me. As George had said, he had a keen mind.

Lassitude overtook me. I spent half an hour willing myself to get up and take some ibuprofen. Even though I knew it would help ease my discomfort, I just couldn't make myself get up. Once I took the pills and got moving, I did my regular checks of e-mail and cell phones. No response. No contact.

When I went to bed, I lay awake for quite a while. I hadn't hurt like this since my last freshman football game. I was pounded all game long by a nose tackle who outweighed me by eighty-five pounds. It was the last game of the season, and I never put on the pads again. I concentrated on marching band the next season, a sensible activity to my mind.

At four-thirty in the morning, my fitful sleep was ended by a metal on metal, grinding sound.

I reacted by trying to leap out of bed. I didn't get far before the pain brought back the reality of my fall. I heard footsteps on the roof. The air had stopped circulating as I hobbled outside carrying the huge mag light. The culprit was long gone.

The sides of the cooler were off and a metal bar protruded. The cooler motor surged and ebbed, threatening to burn out. An iron posthole digger was jammed into the squirrel cage, effectively stopping movement.

I shuffled inside and turned off the motor. I thought about calling the sheriff's department yet again, considered all that that would entail, and couldn't face it. My body had had enough. The adrenaline jolt, stuffy air, and pain weren't enough to keep me awake. I slept until almost 8 a.m.

After checking to make sure the cooler had been vandalized—that it wasn't just a nightmare—I called the sheriff's department and reported it. Deputy Mendez, to my chagrin, arrived in short order. He gazed up at the cooler, stroking his mustache, and wondered aloud how he could get up there.

I brought out the ladder and he climbed up. After a perfunctory look at the damage, he came back down. He pulled out his pocket notebook and pen. "Explain why you didn't report this in a timely manner." His chin jutted at me.

I said, "There was no point in it."

His eyes widened. "I'd like to know why not."

"The perpetrator was gone. There are too many places to hide in the dark around here. He wasn't going to be found, just like the other night with the burglary. Plus all I heard were footsteps on the roof. I wasn't in time to see anyone, so I don't have any sort of description. I'm sure whatever physical evidence was left is still there."

"How do you know it was a man if you didn't see him?"

"I don't."

"You said, '*He* wasn't going to be found.'"

"That was just a generic term. 'He or she,' then."

The deputy glared at me. "In the future, just call and let the professionals do their job. Now, has anyone given you trouble, lately?"

"No," I said shortly, missing Sandino. I didn't regard fist-waving by Steve Paasch and mouthed obscenities by Suzie Parker to be trouble.

"Now, think about it," said Mendez. "Don't just dismiss the idea. Most of the time vandalism like this is perpetrated because of real or perceived conflicts."

I wondered what textbook he was quoting, but he had a point. "There is something, but I don't know who has done this. Yesterday those kids who ride around in the pick-up pool seemed upset with me."

"What did they do?" Mendez interrupted.

"Yelled, shook their fists."

"Why?"

"I really don't know. Last night the cooler stopped working."

He interrupted again. "Define 'stopped working.'"

"The air was blowing, but it was warm. When I went out to fix it there were several people hiding in the shadows, but I couldn't see them."

"How do you know they were there?"

"I heard them. A laugh, movement in the weeds, that sort of thing."

"How—?"

I cut him off by holding up my hands in surrender. "Deputy Mendez, I'm trying to help you. I don't need to be cross examined on every statement I make. This is exactly why I didn't call at four-thirty this morning. Really, I'm on your side."

He blinked, cocked his head as if listening to himself, and then allowed a slow grin to lighten his face. "I guess dealing with deception becomes a habit. I apologize. You're absolutely right. When I slip into it again, let me know."

"Absolutely," I said with relief. "Anyway, I fixed the cooler. It was just a wad of wood shavings preventing the water from getting to the pads. I wouldn't have thought it was vandalism except I heard the people in the shadows. In fact, I tried to get a look at them with a mag light, but they were behind that palo verde tree." Even in daylight the tree was so massive and the branches so numerous it was impossible to see into it. "They ran for it and got away before I could see them. If you find some people all scratched up from palo verde thorns, you might question them. I wasn't going to admit to this next part, but since you're so attentive… when I was putting the side back on the cooler, someone threw a rock at me. I dodged but fell off the roof."

Mendez nodded, pursing his lips. "That explains your stiffness when you got the ladder. And you're bent just a little to the right. I gather you survived all right."

"The worst part was having the breath knocked out of me. Panic city."

"Been there. Done that," said Mendez. "Would sitting be more comfortable? I have a few things to tell you when you're through."

"I don't know," I said. There was a bench identical to the one I had sat on yesterday positioned to enjoy the canyon and ridge. I tried to sit, but quickly straightened. "Standing is fine. To finish, I don't know if Steve Paasch and company are involved. And if they are, I can't say I saw them, because I didn't."

"Fair enough. I called the ranger station in Alpine this morning," said Mendez. "No progress. They didn't send anyone as they promised, and the camp host never radioed on his ham radio. They promised to check this morning."

"Okay." I nodded.

"I found an early morning walker who saw the blue RV following the Lexus out Scenic Loop, Tuesday morning early. So we know it exists, but we have no license plate." He watched me as I winced with pain. "You might consider going to the doctor. He can give you something stronger than ibuprofen if you need it, and we can document your injuries in case it comes to a trial. It's up to you. I won't insist. Truthfully, unless we can prove intent, there's not much we can do, even if we find the rock thrower."

Mendez put his hand on the ladder, ready to ascend. "I'm going to check for prints on the iron bar and snap a few pictures. Then I'll check around the palo verde to see what they left. Someone has a reason for the vandalism because they came here in the middle of the night and perpetrated it. Feel free to get the damage repaired or replaced. And disregard what I said yesterday. Keep asking away."

He took two steps up the ladder before I remembered the amber lights in the night sky.

"When I was on the roof last night, I saw some UFOs."

He stopped on the second rung. "They wouldn't have been amber in color, would they? Those are flares for night operations on the gunnery range. Very common and not at all mysterious."

I went inside the house when Mendez finished. He bore away several fingerprints, branches with bits of cloth caught by thorns, and junk food wrappers of the type that had been left near the Lexus. Someone had a reason for the vandalism. Perhaps the Ellsworths were the intended target. Their house had been burgled. Their Lexus had been trashed. Their cooler had been vandalized. And they were missing.

I leafed through the yellow pages and checked online for cooler repairmen. There was nothing promising. Most repairmen were in Casa Grande or the Phoenix area, too far away to be of any use today. I assumed the local people who worked on coolers didn't advertise. Word of mouth was probably sufficient.

I decided to try T.J. Tatum. He sounded half asleep.

I said, "Good morning. You'll never believe what happened last night."

"Did someone get through my lock work and burglarize the Ellsworths again?"

"Worse. They mangled the cooler."

T.J. didn't respond.

"Did you hear what I said?"

"I must still be asleep. I could have sworn you said someone mangled your cooler."

"I did."

"Really? I've never heard of that happening. Isn't there an unwritten rule in Ajo about protecting coolers? Or is it just baseball that has unwritten rules? 'Don't speak about a no-hitter or you'll jinx the pitcher.'"

"I don't know, but if there are, the unwritten rules aren't followed any better than the written ones. Anyway, there is an iron posthole digger jammed into the squirrel cage."

"I think I have wax in my ears. Did you really say 'an iron posthole digger?'"

"Give yourself a gold star. Anyway, I'd be extremely

grateful if you'd come take a look at it. I don't think it can be fixed. I'll need some advice on how to replace it."

"I'll be there in an hour."

I ate some toast in the family room in front of the television, catching up on the news. It took some doing to maneuver into a cushioned chair, but once I was there, I was more comfortable.

I watched a lively debate concerning the failure of the federal government to secure the border with Mexico. This hit a little too close to home.

Beyond that, Arizona news was wall-to-wall fires. There were five small fires, four of them in Cochise County southeast of Tucson, none more than 50% contained. The Toughnut Fire was just south of Tombstone, the Naco Fire was right on the border with Mexico, the Whetstone Fire was in the area of Kartchner Caverns, and the Bear Hollow Fire was deep in the Chiricahua Mountains. The other fire was west of Payson. None of them were near the White Mountains or the Black River.

A meteorologist talked about the tinder-dry conditions of southern Arizona and gave fire safety tips. He said the diminishing winds would allow the firefighters to get the upper hand today on all fires except the Bear Hollow, where winds were still strong. The annual surge of moisture from the Gulf of California wasn't due until July, and so conditions remained ideal for more fires.

Coming out on the lawn where the sun had already cranked up the heat, I disturbed a flock of quail. The birds ran zigzagging in little committees past my truck down the road, scattering as a bicycle came up the driveway. Marco Armendarez, whistling as usual.

The whistling stopped abruptly as he came in sight of the cooler.

"Good morning, Marco," I said.

"My dad sent me by to see if you needed any more help today. Uh, the library has great air conditioning and it opened ten minutes ago." He looked up in disbelief. "What are you gonna do?"

"T.J. is coming over to see if it can be repaired."

"No way, Jose."

"You didn't happen to see Lorenzo again, did you?"

"No."

"I would like to meet some of the band members," I said. "If I'm going to consider putting in for the job, I want to get a feel for the students I would be working with."

"Good idea," said Marco.

"Do you think you can get Steve Paasch or any of the others to come up here?"

"I don't know. They don't like me. The only thing we have in common is band. But I'll try."

"Better yet, get them to go to The Milky Whey and I'll treat. Call me on my cell phone if you can work something out." I gave him the number.

T.J. Tatum arrived as Marco, whistling, rode away on his bicycle. T.J. stared at the roof for a long moment before speaking. Then he said, "I was hoping you were pulling my leg."

"Thank you for coming."

"I don't think I've ever seen that done to an evaporative cooler. You could be right. It may be more cost effective just to replace it, but let me make a start and see what needs to be done."

The phone rang. I went inside and answered. Gladys Takamine, breathless, said, "Shibasaburo has fallen. He's okay, but I'm going to need help getting him back on his feet."

T.J. and I dashed next door, finding the front door wide open and Gladys beside Shibasaburo, who was prone, an aluminum walker lying partially beneath his body.

I took one arm and shoulder while T.J. took the other, explaining to Shibasaburo what we were going to do. He nodded his head, but his words were slurred and unintelligible. T.J. looked across at me and said, "Let's do it."

Gladys handed her husband the walker, but T.J. intercepted it, bending it back into shape while supporting Shibasaburo.

Shibasaburo stood there, dazed. He might have fallen again, but we assisted him to his chair. I asked Gladys what she was doing out of bed.

"I'm following doctor's orders and keeping quiet. That's why I called. The nurse already left and you were closer."

When all of us were seated, T.J. asked if Shibasaburo was always like this. "Should we call a doctor?"

Gladys shook her head. "Some days are better than others, and this isn't one of the good ones. His condition is the result of an auto accident. His legs were crushed, and his head injuries permanently affected his speech. He regained partial use of his legs, but speech therapy never got him back to normal. Now his speech is deteriorating again. He thinks quite clearly, but he can't express his thoughts. Partial paralysis makes writing and typing impossible. He had to relearn how to eat and read, and do many commonplace things. His abilities were just erased from his brain. He regained most of them quickly, but communication is a problem."

We assisted Shibasaburo down the hall to his

bedroom. It was apparent that he spent most of his time bedridden, but a television, radio, CD player, and a book close at hand argued in favor of his wife's assessment that his mental faculties were still healthy.

As we walked back to the Ellsworth's, T.J. said, "What's wrong with you? You were in pain when we lifted Shibasaburo."

I admitted to falling off the roof, going into more detail on my night.

"Somebody really wanted that cooler out of commission. What's to stop them from doing it again tonight?"

"Good question," I said.

Sandino's white sedan was parked next to our two trucks and Sandy was walking back from the front door.

"Don't bother ringing the doorbell," she said, her eyes twinkling. "No one is home."

T.J. went back to cooler repair while Sandy came inside, where it was stuffy but not as hot as outside.

As Sandy and I sat in the living room, I filled her in on my night and Mendez's investigation.

Sandy consulted a pocket notebook. "I just got a report from the Border Patrol. They finally caught up with the undocumented aliens they tracked from the Lexus, but they had to go practically to Gila Bend. Nothing on your aunt and uncle. Eleven UDAs, eight adults and three children. They stole the Lexus from the ranch, as we suspected. They claim they never saw Bart and Betty. They said when they abandoned the car in the arroyo, only the driver's side window and steering column were broken. The man who claimed to be the driver had a hand injury that accounts for the blood at the ranch. He bashed in the window with a rock, but he hit it so hard his hand went through the glass. He has quite a laceration."

"Do agents believe their story?"

Sandy nodded. "This is not the first time they have caught the driver. They're convinced he didn't know anything about the trashing of the car until they told him. Now he's scared he will get the blame, but all the UDAs tell the same story."

"At least they didn't attack Betty and Bart."

"I have now interviewed Rodney Zamecki and Steve Paasch, and I have been able to reconstruct what happened here. Rodney readily admits coming up here to get food. He won't say who told him the Ellsworths were gone or who told him the key was taped to a yellow note on the front door. He saw the damage in the office and vehemently denies any involvement with that."

I asked how she could believe anything he said.

"Rodney tells the truth. He's not creative enough to lie. He refuses to admit certain things, but when he says something, it's the truth as he knows it. When he came up here Tuesday the office was already trashed. He didn't notice it for awhile because he spent most of his time in the kitchen. When he noticed it, he panicked and got out. Wednesday night he found he still had the key and decided to come back for a midnight snack. When he finished eating he looked around the office, beaming his flashlight around. A stack of books toppled—I'm sure he knocked it down—making a loud noise. He looked around a little longer before he realized someone might have heard the noise. When he saw the flashing lights of the patrol cars, he ran for it, leaving the door open and losing his hat in the orange tree."

"What did Steve say?" I asked.

"He flat out denies everything. He was never here, he had no contact with Zam—that's what he calls Rodney—he knows nothing about a key, he was in Phoenix when the Lexus was vandalized, etcetera. But he's just the opposite of Rodney. If he says it, it's probably a lie. Based on the fact that he and Rodney hang out together and he isn't above getting his friends in trouble, I'll bet Steve had a hand in the vandalism and possible burglary in the office. Then he tried to deflect blame by taping the key to the note and getting Rodney to come up here."

"How do you suppose he got the key?"

"He's too observant for his own good. It could have been any of a thousand ways." Sandy shifted uncomfortably. "Steve has it in for you. He was adamant that I should investigate you. Now I know it is simply a ploy to turn my attention away from him, but he may try to frame you or even attack you in the guise of trying to locate 'his friend' Bishop Ellsworth."

"Is there a special relationship between the two?"

"Nothing that I know of, although Bart tried to be a father figure to him. Steve never knew his birth father. His mother is in and out of prison. The only stability he's known is his grandparents here, but they don't have the strength or insight to keep him in line. Steve constantly refers to Bishop Ellsworth as his scoutmaster, which he was briefly, but in the end Bart had to ask him to leave the troop since he refused to follow the rules." Sandy stood, ready to depart.

Leaving the front door ajar, we stopped and talked to T.J. for a moment beside his truck. The sun was beating down and the temperature soaring. T.J. said, "Why did the wind have to stop? That was the only thing keeping the temperature moderate."

Sandy said, "The weatherman said 110° today, 115° tomorrow, and 120° Sunday."

"Better make that trip to the Yukon," I advised T.J. "Can't you at least work in the shade?"

"Speaking of the wind," said Sandy, "I've asked the Voluntary Independent Posse to start a search for Betty's note, apparently lost in the wind. The VIPs are volunteers who get training and help the sheriff's department. The note could be anywhere, stuck to a cactus, picked up by a packrat, anything. They will start on this western slope, since the winds have been from the east."

The phone rang. Two phones, in fact. As I dashed into the house, I noticed T.J. answering his cell phone.

Chapter thirteen

"Ted, this is Ellen Kramer." I recognized the voice of the Ellsworth's youngest daughter, who lived in Payson. "The forest rangers didn't check for my parents like they said they would! They waited for the camp host to radio, and he didn't do it. It would have taken them no time at all. Instead I have to spend a whole day doing it myself. Sorry, don't mean to yell at you."

"I share your sentiments," I said. "So when are you leaving?"

"Actually, I checked first thing this morning and we're already on the road entering Heber now."

"Who do you have with you?"

"My children. My husband is a forest ranger, but he has a high mucky-muck from Washington coming in today concerning that wildfire west of us. He's got to be there."

"How soon will you be able to check for Betty and Bart?"

"It'll be afternoon before we get there, but we won't be able to contact you till later. I'll try to call from Big Lake, but sometimes coverage is spotty there. It may be evening before I can reach you. If they're not in their usual spot, I intend to check the whole area."

"Hopefully you'll find them right where you expect and it'll be all over. If not, I have a thought." There was a crackle of poor reception. "You're breaking up," I said.

"Go ahead. I can hear you fine."

"If we haven't located your parents by Sunday, won't they attend church?"

"You're right! I can leave word in Eager. Also, I've got a wedding reception I have to attend tomorrow. I won't be able to come down until Sunday afternoon if we haven't found them by then. I'm really sorry."

"Don't worry. We're doing all we can to locate them, Ellen. Ellen? Are you there?"

Reception had terminated.

Almost immediately the phone rang, again. "Ellen," I said.

"No," said a deep male voice. "This is George Ellsworth." The oldest son. The summer school teacher.

"Good morning," I said. "I was just talking to your sister and we got cut off. She's on the way to Buffalo Crossing. The rangers dropped the ball and didn't check on your parents."

"Listen, I just have a few minutes between classes. I went through Dad's emails last night. He mentioned family history a lot, and said in one that he was going to get professional researching help. About three weeks ago, Dad was agitated because he had to take his truck to the shop to have a new motor put in. He never said it was done, but he also never complained that it wasn't."

"Did he say what shop and where?"

"No. I assume it is in Ajo."

"I'll do some checking," I said.

T.J. and Sandy were chatting when I came back outside. T.J. looked up. "I've got to go open a car. The Dalmatian locked inside refuses to open the door."

I laughed.

"On the brighter side, I can repair the cooler if I can find the right parts. While I'm gone I'll stop at the hardware store."

"Go rescue the dog," I said. "I can wait."

T.J. turned to Sandy. "Drag Ted to the library if his brain starts to fry. They have great air conditioning."

As T.J. got in his truck, Sandy turned a critical eye on me. She said, "But how will I know if his brain starts to fry?" I gave Sandy a mock scowl.

T.J. rolled down his window before he eased down the driveway. "Ted, no wonder you fell. That roof is a bear, even in full sun."

"You fell off the roof?" said Sandy.

"I told you about my night."

"You didn't mention falling off the roof. It's too late, T.J. His brain is already sautéed."

"And you call yourself a detective. You just had to read between the lines."

"Did you get a doctor's appointment?"

"Mendez said I didn't have to."

"Is that an exact quote?"

"Well, not exactly. He did recommend it, but mainly for pain control, not that it would be needed as evidence."

"He's concerned about pain? What about your cracked skull?"

"I landed on my feet, I'll have you know," I said. "Anyway, I'm going to try calling Bob Ellsworth again right now, if you're interested. And if you come inside I'll tell you what Ellen and George had to say."

Sandy came inside and listened to my report.

After there was no answer again on Bob's private line, I got through to the Denver restaurant. I explained to the woman who answered why I needed to contact Bob Ellsworth, pushing the speaker button so Sandy could hear the reply.

The prissy soprano voice said, "Sir, the Great Roberto isn't here right now. May I take a message?"

"I left a message last night. Do you know if he got it?"

"Sir, I wasn't on duty, so I wouldn't have any idea. Would you care to leave another message?"

"Can you tell me when Bob, the Great Roberto, will be in?"

"That's privileged information. I'm not allowed to give that out."

"As I've explained," I said, "his parents are missing, and we think it is possible he is on vacation."

"I'm sure I don't know what he does on his own time. All I can tell you is that he isn't here."

"Can you at least confirm that he is on vacation?"

"No, sir, that is privileged information. I'd really like to help you, but I'm not allowed to give out that type of information over the phone. Can you come down in person?"

"I'm more than six hundred miles away," I said dryly.

"I'm sorry. There's nothing—"

"Just a minute, please," I said forcefully, interrupting her before she hung up. "I can appreciate your rules, and I respect them, but can't you make an exception? His parents are missing, there has been a burglary at their home, and their car has been found abandoned and vandalized. I think this is cause for concern, don't you?

We need to talk to Bob."

"This is a busy restaurant—"

"Could you at least let me talk to a supervisor?"

"I don't know who you are or who you think you are," she said in a cold fury, "but don't call back. I *am* the supervisor." Click.

I looked at Sandy in dismay. "Well, I blew that."

"Nonsense. You handled yourself very well. I'd have lost my temper long before she hung up. Let me try."

She pushed redial and in a moment was talking to prissy voice. Sandy said sweetly, "May I speak with the manager, please?" She put it on speaker so that I could hear.

Prissy voice, showing no trace of fury, said, "May I ask what your concern is?"

"I recently ate at your restaurant, and I want to tell the manager how much I enjoyed the meal. In particular, I want to compliment your chef, the Great Roberto."

"Please hold."

"She was lying to me!" I said hotly.

Sandy smiled. "People do lie."

"When did you ever eat there?"

"Three years ago while attending a training conference. That restaurant is one of the best in Denver."

A different female voice came on the line. "This is Jane McNary. May I be of assistance?"

"I'm afraid I misled your secretary somewhat, and I apologize. I ate at your restaurant three years ago and enjoyed it, but what I really want to talk to you about is your chef, Bob Ellsworth. I'm a detective with the sheriff's department in Ajo, Arizona."

McNary's voice wasn't quite as friendly. "I haven't hung up because I'm aware Bob is from Ajo, but please realize that over the phone, it is impossible to know who you really are. We've had a lot of trouble with people bothering our chefs at home, so we don't give out personal information."

"I understand," said Sandy, "and I can go through the Denver police to get the information, but that takes time that we may not have." She glibly dropped a few names and personal details of the chief of police and several prominent officers, and soon McNary's voice began to thaw.

She said, "Robert is on vacation, but as far as I know he is at home here in Denver. In fact, the reason for the vacation was so he could move into a new house and get everything settled." She gave Sandy his new telephone number.

Sandy asked about the RV, but McNary knew nothing about it. Then she said, "How long has he been on vacation?"

"All week. He worked last Saturday. If you aren't able to catch him at home, he comes back to work Monday evening."

Sandy dialed the number given her by McNary. "Maybe we're making progress." She put the phone on speaker again.

"Hello?"

"Hello," said Sandy. "My name is Mrs. Sandino. May I speak with your mother or father, please?"

We could hear the close ticking of a clock, a more distant television, and barely discernable water running in the pipes. Suddenly the sound of a door opening and closing came over the speaker. A masculine voice said very loudly, "Who's left the phone off the hook? Barbara!" The phone clicked off.

Sandy hit the redial button. "Hello?" said the same masculine voice, still perturbed.

"Bob, this is Blanca Sandino in Ajo."

"Blanca!" His agitation was gone immediately. "It's great to hear your voice. Boy, it's been forever."

"You moved, what, seven or eight years ago?"

"I've been back to visit three or four times, but I have never run into you."

"That's a good thing since I now work in law enforcement."

Bob asked what was on her mind.

"Your parents. They had a housesitter coming so they could leave for the summer, but they disappeared before he got here. Have you heard anything?"

"No, I've been tied up getting the builders to finish the house on schedule, getting moved in, and changing my phone number. I haven't even had time to tell everyone what it is, so I've been out of touch. When I got into the celebrity chef business I had no idea how people would react. It's like I'm a movie star. My fans won't let us have any private family time."

"So business is good?"

"Yeah, but family comes first. You build up your name to get recognized to earn a decent living, but then you have to go into hiding to escape your fans. It's a vicious circle. So how can I help?"

"I think you've already given me the answer to my biggest question. Your brother Scott said you were buying a new RV, and he thought—"

Bob started laughing. "I told Scott we were staying in an RV while the work on the house was being finished. I may have said I wanted to buy it, because I really did like it, but that was never an option. I don't care how much money he thinks I make, believe me, there is no way I could build a house and buy an RV at the same time."

"Do you have any thoughts on where your parents could be?"

"They're not at Buffalo Crossing?" he asked.

"Your sister Ellen is driving over from Payson right now. The rangers didn't get over to check yesterday."

"I can't imagine them camping anywhere else. The only other thing that comes to mind is an emergency of some sort."

Sandy shook her head. "We've checked all the hospitals—"

Bob laughed, interrupting Sandy again. "In my dad's eyes, an emergency is finding somebody who needs help. He and Mom would drop everything and go help. Do you have time for a story?"

Sandy looked at me. I nodded my assent. "Sure," she said.

"Once on vacation we found an old Cadillac off to the side of the road. Sitting inside refusing to leave was an old guy who said he didn't want to abandon his car. He was sure it would start when the engine got cool enough. He turned the key, but the engine wouldn't turn over. Dad suggested filling the radiator to see if that would help. He tried, but the water went straight through the radiator to the ground. Even then it took Dad half an hour to talk the guy into accepting a ride and sending a tow truck. Mind you, he was red as an Ajo Red Raider jersey and looked like a candidate for heat stroke. When he finally agreed to be rescued, I threw his luggage in our car. Dad got him settled in front of the air conditioner and made him drink a Gatorade. He saved the man's life. I'll bet what happened is Dad got wind of something that required his immediate attention. He knew Ted would understand."

Sandy thanked him and hung up. She said, "One by one our theories are biting the dust."

"If Bob is right," I said, "all we have to do is wait. By the way, why did you call yourself Blanca?"

"That's what everybody called me all through school. I didn't get nicknamed Sandy until after my marriage to Jose Sandino. The guys at the sheriff's station started calling me that because of my name, obviously not from the color of my hair."

Sandy stood up, ready to get on with her day. I accompanied her out, asking if she had any thoughts on protecting the cooler from further mischief.

"We can have the deputies check the area several times a night, but a determined vandal could still find a way. How did he get on the roof? Did he use the ladder?"

"I don't think so. I found it put away each time."

We walked around the house looking. The fig tree grew on one corner close to the roof. It had a stout enough trunk and branches that it was a likely candidate. Sandy found broken branches and leaves where someone had climbed up and gotten on the roof. She suggested rigging an alarm so that I could call the sheriff's department when the vandal was in the act.

Sandy's cell phone rang as we walked to her car. I backed off to give her some privacy. When she finished she came over and said, "They've got a Spanish speaker at the station who needs to be interviewed. I have to go." Seeing that my hopes were rising, she shook her head. "Nothing to do with the Ellsworths, at least that's what they think at this point. But you never know."

I walked back to the deep shade of the chinaberry

tree and watched Sandy drive down the hill. So she was married. No wonder I felt so free and easy around her. She hadn't mentioned a divorce or in any way indicated she was free to date. Good. I needed time to heal from the wounds left by Janet.

While I watched, T.J. Tatum's tiny pickup passed Sandy's sedan and he was soon levering himself out of the confining space.

I said, "Did you save the dog?"

"No problem. That lady will have a cleaning bill, though. That dog slobbered all over everything. The hardware store had everything I needed, too."

"Great," I said, paying him on the spot for the parts. I tried to add some extra for labor, but he would have none of that. I continued, "I have some more phone calls to make and then I'll be free to help you. I still haven't reached the Ellsworth's veterinarian. I don't think, now, that anything has happened to the dogs, but I need to confirm it. Also, I want to check with auto repair shops. George Ellsworth said Bart was having the motor replaced in his truck."

T.J. nodded, getting back to work.

Returning to the office, I quickly found the vet's phone number on file and made the call. The vet was busy, so I left my cell phone number.

I used the landline to call auto shops while I waited. There were a surprising number of them for such a small town, and each place mentioned someone who did work at his home. The ones I talked to knew nothing about the truck.

The vet soon called back. She had had no recent contact with the Ellsworths or their golden retrievers.

On the off chance that Ellen Kramer was in the area

of Big Lake as she checked the Ellsworth's usual camping spot, I called her cell phone. It wasn't in the service area.

I took some water and a snack out to T.J., and then helped him on the roof as a go-fer while he finished the repairs.

After cool air began circulating in the house, T.J. drove off.

Then I went directly to the fence and waved my arms, trying to get Manny Molina's attention. He came toward me with such a grim, forbidding expression that I thought he was going to attack.

Chapter fourteen

I offered my hand over the fence, but instead of shaking, Manny Molina just stared at me. I introduced myself. He watched me intently, and then said, "Manny Molina," his countenance still hostile. His voice was normal and he had a breathy accent. I later learned that this was characteristic of the Tohono O'odham tribe. He was so adept at lip reading I soon forgot he was deaf.

He smelled like pesticide, reminding me of my dad coming in to change clothes after spraying the garden. He asked if we had located the Ellsworths, but his expression still didn't change.

"No," I said, "every idea is a dead end. All we really know is that they were last seen driving up the canyon followed by a large blue RV Tuesday morning."

Manny stared. "I saw the RV," he said. "It came to McBain's house."

"This was Tuesday morning early?"

He nodded. "About five."

"Can you describe the van?"

"I can draw it."

I readily agreed. "Did you notice the license plate?"

"Colorado." He rattled off the numbers and letters, which I jotted on the card Sandy had given me after the burglary.

"How did you happen to memorize those numbers?"

"You take eyes for granted. I don't."

"Who was in the RV?"

"A young white guy going bald. He had a mustache. I can draw him, too. There was also a woman, but I didn't get a good look at her."

"Did you talk to the man?"

Manny nodded. "He asked for Ellsworths. I directed him."

Manny hadn't gotten the driver's name. He answered my questions, but he was not friendly. When I headed to the house to get some paper and pens for his drawings, he vaulted the fence easily and accompanied me. On the way I asked him about vacuuming the pool. He said it was an automatic system and told me where to find the switch.

I left him in the office sketching swiftly. I got a recent Ellsworth family photograph from the dining room and my trumpet from my bedroom. I returned to find that he was gifted not only in music and gardening, but in art as well. The pictures had come to life. The vehicle and man were easily identifiable. In fact, the balding man seemed very familiar. Where had I seen him?

I showed Manny the family group shot. He took his time studying it, but then shook his head.

I told him I was thinking of organizing a community band for the summer. This was true. Sandy, Marco Armendarez, and Debbie Piccioli would be interested. If I had met four talented musicians in less than forty-eight hours, I imagined that getting a band together wouldn't be too difficult. I asked Manny to play in it as I tried to hand him my trumpet. He backed away from my shiny silver instrument.

"I had a long talk with Gladys Takamine," I said, "and she told me what a good trumpet player you are."

"Was!" said Manny fiercely. "It's over. It's been too long since I played. I have no time for it."

"'If you lose your leisure, look out, you may lose your soul,'" I quoted.

"I get plenty of leisure. I sleep five or six hours a night."

"Benjamin Franklin said, 'There will be sleeping enough in the grave.'"

Manny kept a grim expression, but I thought I saw him suppress the beginnings of a smile. "You may win a battle of quotations, but that won't make it possible for me to hear."

"But you kept playing in high school, even after the operation. Gladys said you were still the best musician in the band."

"That was because of Mr. Schneider. He had such an expressive face I could tell without thinking what I needed to do. And my playing brought such joy to him that I couldn't quit."

"Give me a chance to take his place."

Manny shook his head. "Your face is too inflexible. Mr. Schneider's face was elastic. He could bend it into any emotion. I could read him. It's easy to read your lips, but your emotions are too quiet. Sorry, it wouldn't work."

I had to take that as his final answer. "Well, if you change your mind, come and get this trumpet. And thank you for the pictures. This could be the breakthrough we need to find the Ellsworths."

As we walked to the door, he said, "I hope you find them. Bart Ellsworth gave me my first break when I started my landscaping business. He gave me a list of trees he wanted and let me do the layout. People saw what I could do and began to hire me."

Manny returned to McBain's, his shoulders a little slumped. I wondered if he regretted turning me down. I might still do the community band for the summer, but it wouldn't be the same challenge without Manny. Music could lift the spirits not only of the audience, but of the musicians. Manny needed it. He was too grim. His almost-smile gave me hope that he would come around, however.

I walked out to the pool. The switch was easy to find once I knew where to look. I flipped it and started the vacuum. Leaving the automatic system going, I drove the drawings and license number to the sheriff's office. Sandy was still translating, so I left them for her.

On the way back, I checked T.J.'s RV just to verify that my memory was correct and that it wasn't the one in the drawing. I also stopped at the hardware store and purchased an inexpensive security alarm, a loud audible alarm. I installed it in the fig tree where it would be tripped for sure.

Manny's statement, "It's been too long since I played," reminded me of my own obligation to practice. When I got indoors, unable to think of anything else to do right then toward finding Betty and Bart, I practiced in the family room. I had brought my flute, clarinet, and trumpet. After I had been playing for well over an hour and was really warmed up, I attacked my personal nemesis: "Scherzo for Trumpet" by Bolero, with its difficult runs and fingering combinations. When I had stopped massacring the piece, the doorbell rang.

On the porch was a young Native American lady with long braided hair, black eyes, and acne scars on her temples. She held her arm awkwardly at her belt as if it were hurt. It was covered by a plastic bag.

She said formally, "Hello, I'm Maria Tirado. I sell tortillas to the Ellsworths, and I was wondering if you would like me to continue delivering during the summer." Her breathy accent was similar to Manny's.

The bag on her arm contained huge flour tortillas. I hesitated, considering this unexpected offer. She continued, "I deliver once a week, every Friday, and the tortillas are homemade, as fresh as you can buy anywhere, only $2.50 a dozen."

"How did you know the Ellsworths were gone?"

"Last Friday when I delivered, Betty said they would be going sometime this week. She didn't know if you would be interested in getting tortillas or not."

Swallowing my disappointment, I asked, "So they didn't call the day they left?"

"No."

"Did Betty say where they were going?"

"Just camping and visiting their children all summer."

Everyone in town knew they were missing, but no one seemed to know their current whereabouts or why they had left early. I agreed to try a dozen tortillas. When I reached for my wallet, I stood my trumpet on its bell on the carpet.

"Was that you playing the trumpet?" she asked. "I thought it was a CD. I just stood here enjoying it until the song was over."

"Thank you," I said, having long ago learned not to

give away my own opinion of the mistakes I had made. "You know who else is really good? Manny Molina. Do you know him?"

"The landscape artist?" she said, her eyes round. "No, I didn't know." She gave me her phone number so that I could place an order for next Friday if I liked the tortillas.

I laid the bag on the dining room table and continued practicing until my cell phone rang. I fumbled the phone in my haste to answer, hoping it was Bart or Betty. No such luck.

It was Marco.

"I found Steve's group, but only Steve wants to meet with you. And you know what?"

"Every one of them is all scratched up."

"How did you know?"

"Wild guess."

"You know more than you're telling me."

"Are you going to The Milky Whey?"

"We'll be there in five minutes."

"On my way."

Both boys were seated at a table in the corner underneath a poster of the Crab Nebula digging into big dippers of ice cream when I arrived.

I stopped at the counter and said, "Hi, Debbie. Was that you I heard practicing your flute last night?"

"You know my name?"

"Detective Sandino told me. She said you really play well, and I agree. The detective plays flute, also."

"How did you hear me?"

"I was sitting outside at the Ellsworth's."

"Oh, that's just up the hill from my house. What can I get you?"

"How about Black Hole Walnut? And I'm paying for Marco's and Steve's as well."

"How do you remember names so well? Little dipper again?"

I nodded. "I'm a high school teacher."

When I paid her, I said, "I may put together a community band this summer. Are you interested?"

Debbie nodded. "Are you going to be our new band director?"

"I'm considering applying for it. That's why I'm meeting Steve."

She said, "If you can handle him, you'll have no trouble with the rest of the band."

When I sat down with the boys, Steve said, "So are you the California guy?"

"Actually, I'm from Wyoming," I said. "I just worked in California. But if I move here I will be the Arizona guy. What kind of ice cream did you get?"

Marco said, "Van Allen Vanilla. 'So much taste it's radioactive.'"

Steve said, "Rocket Road. So are you taking over the band?"

"I'm considering applying for the job," I said. "That's why I wanted to meet you."

Steve's right hand was bandaged, and he had multiple scratches on his arms and face, many of them visible through his scraggly red beard. The one on his forehead was four inches long, and it hadn't completely scabbed over.

I said, "What happened to you?"

"It's nothing. I snagged my hand on a rusty nail cleaning Mrs. Watson's shed. I had to get a testosterone shot."

Marco rocked back and forth, biting his knuckles, making no sound.

"And all the scratches?"

"In Mrs. Watson's yard. She had me take out a sticker bush and it fought back. I got that real deep one when I was unloading at the dump. I pulled and it snapped right into my face." There were no scratches on his palms.

I didn't believe him for a second, but a public place like this wasn't the best place to worm the truth out of him.

"So, what do you think, Steve?" I said. "Can you still play the drums?"

Steve rapped out a quick cadence with his hands on the table. "No problemo."

"Good. I'm wondering if there is enough interest to form a community band for the summer."

Steve said, "Count me in."

Marco said, "Me, too."

"Do you think we can find enough willing musicians?"

The boys named eight or ten students and adults they thought would be interested.

"Good," I said. "Sounds like we have enough interest to start spreading the word, but I won't actually begin practice until I locate the Ellsworths and confirm they are okay."

Steve said, "So how come you got their house?"

"They asked me to housesit for the summer."

"So it's not really your house."

"Of course not."

"And you're just there to protect it? Not doing a very good job, are you?"

Marco laughed. "Sorry," he said to me.

Steve said, "Well, if the shoe fits, walk a mile in it. Burglary, vandalism. On his watch."

"What did you hear about the burglary and vandalism?" I asked him. "For that matter, what do you know about the disappearance of the Ellsworths?"

"Nothing. I don't hear anything. I don't know anything about any of that. You're as bad as Sandino. She leaned on me last night like you wouldn't believe."

"*Mrs.* Sandino," I corrected.

"What makes either of you think I know anything about it?"

"I've seen you all over in that pick-up pool. I got the impression that you know everyone and everything. Am I wrong?"

"I do know a lot, but not about the Ellsworths." Steve fixed his eyes on me. "You're the one who knows everything about the Ellsworths."

"What are you insinuating?"

"I don't even know that word. I'm saying you know what happened to the Ellsworths." He turned to Marco. "He comes to town and then they disappear. He takes over their house. It's as plain as the night is long."

Marco just shook his head.

Steve continued, "So what about it, Mr. White? What happened to my scoutmaster and his wife? Has Sandino questioned you, too? What's your alias?"

"Why do you want to be in the community band if you think I'm responsible for the Ellsworth's disappearance? You don't really suspect me, do you?"

"I *know* you're responsible, and I told Sandino too."

"*Mrs.* Sandino."

"Sandino," said Steve, dropping his spoon into his empty bowl.

"Steve, you can't go around making accusations without evidence."

"How do you know I don't have any evidence?"

"Because I didn't do it. The Ellsworths were last seen driving out Scenic Loop early Tuesday morning followed by a blue RV. I didn't arrive until Wednesday afternoon."

"They were here. I'll bet no one saw them because they stayed home."

"How did they get back home? They were driving the Lexus, which was vandalized out at their ranch, so it never returned."

"Someone gave them a lift."

"With the whole town in an uproar over their disappearance, why didn't they say something?"

"The people who gave them a ride probably went to Rocky Point and don't know about that."

Marco said, "Steve, that's just stupid."

"Oh, yeah? Mr. White has hoodwinked you. He's a fraud, a Charlemagne, a conman. See? I have a vocabulary, too."

"So why did you agree to meet him? Just for the ice cream?"

"Just watch, Marco. When he gets put in jail, you'll go to juvie for aiding and bedwetting."

Steve stood, pushing back his chair. "As for you, Mr. Band Director, don't think you're out of the forest till the fat lady sings. We'll get the goods on you, even if we have to—" He clamped his mouth shut.

"Have to what?" I asked.

"Just go back home, California Guy." Steve stomped toward the door. He clipped a table and knocked it down with a ker-thunk. He left without taking notice.

Debbie Piccioli came around the counter, but Marco

and I righted the table before she got there.

She said, "You stood up to Steve! That's something Dr. Wilcox never did. Steve will get the message."

Back at the corner table, Marco said, "Did you notice Steve didn't turn on you until his ice cream was gone?"

"This is delicious black walnut," I said, taking a bite.

"Black Hole Walnut," said Marco. "Steve lied to you."

"Probably more than once."

"I've heard him use that line about cleaning Mrs. Watson's shed at least twenty times. It hasn't been touched in three years."

"I'm not surprised."

"That doesn't explain how the rest of his group got all scratched up, too. So how come you knew about it? What aren't you telling me?"

"It doesn't sound like any of them will be in the community band, does it?" I said.

"Can we do the band without drums?"

"Surely they aren't the only percussionists in town."

"Adults don't play drums."

"You'd be surprised. Most drummers grow up."

Marco gave me his patented frowning smirk. "On another subject, did you know there are some spectacular fires in Cochise County?"

"I saw some coverage this morning."

"Not later?"

"No."

"At noon they showed the Bear Hollow fire in the Chiricahuas. The fire is so big and hot it just engulfed a tree and the whole thing ignited. All at once. Poof! A huge ponderosa pine. We never have fires like that here."

"Good," I said. "That's another plus for Ajo."

"Another reason to get out of California."

"So after meeting Steve, what do you think?"

"He'll be a challenge. He needs someone who cares."

"But how much difference can one teacher make?"

"That is the right question."

Marco had to leave for supper. I went to Copper Café since I was already at the Plaza. Two days in a row I had ice cream before dinner. Not a good habit.

Copper Café was tastefully decorated with copper pots and pans, paintings depicting the desert around Ajo, and potted plants. I had no sooner gotten seated than Sandy, looking wilted, entered the café. She spotted me and came over. We ordered before I asked if she had gotten the pictures and license plate provided by Manny Molina.

"The plate returns to Handicapped Rentals of Colorado, which refused to give me any information over the phone, the stinkers. I've contacted my friends in Denver PD to find out who rented the RV. That'll take some time."

"Did your translating job have anything to do with the Ellsworths?" I asked.

"No, it was a family looking for a lost UDA. He crossed illegally two weeks ago and never made it to his destination. It's really sad. I couldn't offer them any hope. We find bodies all too often, but that's not something to talk about at dinner. How is your pondering going? Have you decided to teach music here?"

I laughed, making the dimple appear in Sandy's left cheek. "The jury is still out. Marco just reminded me of two reasons to leave California, wildfires and earthquakes."

"Mudslides?"

"Make that three. Marco and Debbie would be great to have in the band. I heard Debbie practicing last night. She's as good as you said. And I really want to work with Steve."

"He needs someone like you."

"Someone, but not necessarily me. I met him over at The Milky Whey." I shook my head. "He has taken a dislike to me. At this point he won't even stay in the band. He knows I know he was under the palo verde tree last night. I asked him about his scratches."

"He didn't admit it, did he?"

"No. I didn't challenge his lies, but I think he sensed I didn't buy them. He made some veiled threats."

Dinner came. I had Chicken Ajo, a chicken breast soaked in lemon juice marinade topped with melted Swiss cheese, and Sandy had taco salad.

"I called Ellen earlier but didn't get through," I said. "She should be calling any time now."

My cell phone rang with my default ring tone, "Hawaii Five-O." I cut off the tympani, my favorite part, in my haste to answer.

Ellen Kramer said, "I'm sorry, Ted, but we didn't find Mom and Dad. We went to Buffalo Crossing first. They aren't camped there. We never saw the camp host, either, but at least his rig is there. Then we went to every campground and fishing spot we've ever visited. It took hours. Nothing. Any progress there?"

I gave her a rundown of the events in Ajo.

She said, "We're exhausted, and the kids are getting crabby. And we're barely in the Show Low area. I was hoping all day I might be able to break away and come down tomorrow, but I don't see how." I assured her I'd keep searching on my end, and we said goodbye.

As we ate, Sandy and I talked about getting a community band going for the summer. "Marco and Debbie want to join. How about you?"

"Too bad I don't have a flute."

"Yeah," I said, "but I know someone who might lend you one."

Back home I checked the fig tree. The alarm was set. I locked the doors and went to bed. I couldn't keep my eyes open, but my brain went on thinking. While in this state in which my body appeared to be asleep but my mind was still wide awake, I felt the air pressure change, as if an outside door had been opened. I didn't hear a sound, but I knew that I was not alone in the house. I didn't move.

Several minutes passed. Just when I was beginning to think I was mistaken, I caught a whiff of the pungent odor of pesticide, reminding me of my dad. The association was so powerful that I cracked my eyelids to see the dark shape of my father coming to tuck me in. The dark shape instead checked around the room and finally opened the closet door. It picked up something equally dark, and eased out of the room without a sound.

After the changing air pressure announced that the intruder was gone, I felt around for my trumpet, which I had placed with my other instruments in the closet. It was gone.

Chapter fifteen

The church was packed with smiling men and tearful women. The pipe organ filled every nook with the "Bridal Chorus" by Wagner. Janet Johnson, radiant in white, walked up the aisle. She stepped in place beside me. She smiled her 'I've waited all my life for this moment and you are the most special man in the world' smile.

The minister said what he said.

Janet said, "I do."

I said, "I do."

The minister said, "I now pronounce you…." He started laughing.

He laughed without stopping for breath. The laughter rolled out of him. Tears squeezed out of his eyes from his mirth. He couldn't stop his maniacal laughter. His face elongated and his mouth opened wider and wider as the laughter deepened.

The tears grew into translucent super balloons that distorted the scene. The colors ran together like a watercolor in the rain, draining away into blackness.

The minister still didn't breathe. Janet joined him in laughter. Her finger, mocking me, blurred.

The minister's enlarging mouth swallowed his entire body. He was gone. Only blackness remained.

Janet's finger disappeared. Then her hand, her arm, indeed her entire body liquefied into blackness. The black liquid covered me. I couldn't breathe. I had to reach the surface in order to breathe. I kicked. Where was the top? Where was the air? Why was the laughter getting louder? If I didn't reach the top instantly I would drown. I gave one last kick.

I awoke sweating, tangled into immobility in the sheet. The laughter wasn't just a dream. It continued. Pounding. Maniacal. Familiar.

I remembered hearing something similar when I was setting up for a concert in Greenwood City—a laugh box. Kids used them along with stink bombs to disrupt classrooms.

I stepped into the hall, but the sound was centered in my bedroom. It was coming from the closet. I emptied the closet, looking for the palm-sized transmitter, finding instead that my trumpet had been returned.

These efforts only succeeded in increasing the volume of the insane laughter by taking away the clothing that muffled it. It was now threatening to curdle my brain.

Still the noise came from the closet, even though it was empty. I shined a flashlight into the closet to see what I had missed, locating a door knob on the back wall. It was locked. I went around to the other side of the door in the master bedroom, finding only blank wall. There was no sign that there ever had been a door.

In that room the laughter was somewhat muted. In the living room it was down to a whisper. In the bedroom across the hall from the family room it couldn't be heard at all.

Unable to find a key, I gave up. I retired to the hall bedroom and tried to get back to sleep.

I kept imagining sounds. A branch scraped against the window. Had the wind returned? I got up and checked. The moonlight backlit the scene, but no branch was visible near the window.

After I lay down again, the scraping sound returned. I endured it for perhaps five minutes, then I bounced out of bed and threw open the curtains. The sound stopped.

The sound returned when I got back in bed. This time I crept stealthily to the window. With a surreptitious twitch I parted the curtains. The sound stopped. Nothing was visible. I gazed at the moonlit west lawn for perhaps five minutes. The window and flowerbed were in shadow. There was no movement. I couldn't see anyone. The whole time I was at the window the sound didn't come.

Back in bed. The sound returned! I turned over, determined to get back to sleep. I was only imagining the scraping. Had to be. There was no one out there.

On the verge of finally getting back to sleep I heard raindrops on the roof. Raindrops? How could that be? The moon was bright. There couldn't be any clouds. I thought, 'Imagination, go to sleep!'

The raindrops continued, or was it hail? The sound abated as if the rain was letting up, then it came back in a rush. I had to be dreaming. It didn't rain in Ajo.

After listening for a few minutes I couldn't stand it. I ran to the window. Everything stopped. The night was still.

I walked back through the darkened house to the guest room. The laugh box continued unabated.

There had to be people outside. The laugh box was

not my imagination. The scraping and raindrops had to be real, too. I put on my shoes and got the mag light.

Someone wanted me to step outside to look around. Why? What did he want to happen to me? I felt an itching between my shoulder blades as if a gun was trained on me. I couldn't let the harassment continue, and I couldn't get a reputation for running to the police every time I turned around.

I stepped to the front door, squared my shoulders, and turned the knob. As I swung open the door a loud alarm sounded. I stopped short on the threshold. A dark shape rose from the flowerbed on my right.

A voice yelled, "Run for it! The cops are coming." Four or five people raced across the lawn toward the west wall behind the tool shed.

The alarm continued. It had to be from the fig tree, which was out of sight around the house. As I emerged onto the lawn a man carrying the iron posthole digger ran by me toward the back of the tool shed. I charged after him.

He half-turned and I recognized Steve Paasch. He tried to throw the iron bar like a javelin. It was so heavy, however, that it fell out of his hand backward. This slowed him enough for me to catch up.

I dropped the mag light and tackled him around the knees in true freshman football form. I brought him down flat on his face on the grass. We both lay there, winded.

The scrambling, running sounds of the others receded into nothing.

I hurt. I hadn't fully recovered from my fall from the roof, although I wasn't nearly as sore as I had been early in the day. The boy struggled against my grip on his knees, but I grimly hung on.

"Steve, stop it. I know who you are."

I heard him spit grass out of his mouth. He said, "You can't. It's too dark before the dawn."

"Looks like your friends have deserted you, Steve."

"Friends don't leave you like a rat on a sinking ship, and I'm not Steve."

"I need to talk to you inside."

"So, let me up."

"Not unless you promise not to run off."

"I promise."

"That was too easy. I don't think I trust you."

"Trust me. You know the old saying, 'Love all, trust me.'"

I shifted to a more comfortable position without allowing Steve to get loose. "Lying on the grass is kind of nice, don't you think?" I said. "I haven't done this since I was a kid."

"What about last night?"

"How would you know about last night unless you were here? I didn't tell anyone except Deputy Mendez and Detective Sandino." And T.J. Tatum, I thought.

Steve was silent. He tensed his right leg, but I had such a strong grip on it that it didn't move.

I said, "Don't even think it."

"You're cutting off the circulatory to my toes. They're going dumb."

"Let's see if we can get up without letting you loose, then. If you make a wrong move you can forget about your feet."

I levered myself up by putting weight on him, keeping him immobile.

Steve said, "Hey! That's me under you. Careful."

I got to my feet, still controlling him. "You shouldn't try to get away, then. Like I said, I need to talk to you privately."

I got him to his feet, keeping a firm grip on him, then shifted my grip to his neck. I knew from experience when I was a teenager that this was a most effective tongue-loosener.

I took him to the fig tree, skirting a fallen step ladder, where I reset the alarm. It had helped save the cooler, but it hadn't alerted the neighbors. I was pleased that the deputies hadn't arrived. I could get information from Steve more effectively than they could. They weren't allowed to use pain as a motivator.

I took Steve to the dining room and sat him down. I sat next to him.

"Okay," I said. "Let's start with tonight."

"Is this catnapping?"

"Not a chance. You're going home after our little talk. Straight home. Do not pass go. Do not collect $200."

Steve waved a hand at the bag of tortillas on the table. "Hey, are those from Maria Tirado? Let's eat tortillas."

"You can have as many as you want as long as you answer my questions."

Steve wasted no time in opening the bag. I noted that his beard had sprouted leaves of grass in addition to last night's scratches. The four-inch gash on his forehead had split open during our exertions. It was oozing.

"All right," I said, "what was the point of tonight? A laugh box, suspicious noises, another attempt to disable the cooler. Why?"

Steve took a bite. I let him swallow, but I wouldn't let him take another bite.

I said, "Answer me."

When he didn't answer immediately, I applied some pressure with my right hand on the back of his neck.

"Okay, okay," Steve said. "You won't leave. We're just trying to help you decide to go home. Stop procrastinating the day you go back to California."

"Why?"

"Isn't it obvious by now? No one wants you here."

"With one breath you said you wanted to be in the summer community band and in the next you want me to leave town. Why the change? What's really going on?"

Steve shrugged.

"All right, how did you get the laugh box behind the door in my closet?"

I applied more pressure when he resisted.

Steve jerked away, but I was able to keep the pressure on his neck. "All right!" he said.

I slackened my grip, but not enough for him to even think about escaping.

Steve said, "The key we have fits the door to the basement."

"Basement?"

"Didn't know about it, did you? Bishop Ellsworth had it dug a few years ago. A bunch of us scouts turned up to help him bring in storage items. He planted that big palo verde in front of the door to shield it from discovery. He waters it. That's how it got so big."

"Are you telling me there is an entrance to the basement through the closet in the guest room?"

"Ooh, you're as quick as a giant sloth."

"So you came in the basement, positioned the laugh box behind the closet door, set it off, and waited for me to run out screaming?"

"Well, I didn't figure you'd be scared. I know you well

enough by now. But I thought you'd come out and check the yard."

"What were you going to do?"

Talking was coming easier now that Steve had started confessing. I loosened my grip, but didn't let go.

Steve said, "Lorenzo and Juan were stationed at each door to trip you as you ran out. Then when you were down we were going to deliver a message."

"Are you talking about assault?"

"Nothing crude like that. Psychedelic warfare. You know, playing on your mind."

"So when I didn't come out…"

"The noises and stuff was designed to draw you out."

"How did you know which room I was in?"

"You turned on the light."

"And how did you know every time I was near the curtain?"

"Suzie was watching from a good hiding place. She signaled."

"You had everything covered."

"Except that alarm!"

"Were you really going to attack my cooler again?"

"I didn't figure you'd even try to go on the roof, and if you did you wouldn't be able to fix it till daylight. So it's your own fault I had to take more direct action."

"'Direct action' is one way of putting it," I said. "A more accurate way is 'vandalism.'"

"It didn't work, though," said Steve, starting on his third tortilla. Confession seemed to be fueling his appetite. "How did you get to be friends with everyone in town so fast?"

"What about the rock?"

"We didn't mean for you to fall. I want you to know

that. We were heading back to town when Lorenzo spotted an owl. You have to understand that an owl swooped down and grabbed his puppy when he was a kid. He has a thing against them. He tried to hit it before I could stop him. It was sheer luck that it was aimed at you."

"Bad luck," I said.

"Well, yeah. We don't want you hurt. We just want you to go home. Psychedelic warfare."

"I still don't understand why you want me out of here."

Steve was silent.

I said, "All right, let's go back to Tuesday. As I understand it, Rodney Zamecki came up here because someone told him about the food," I cleared my throat, "which was *left for me*. He was told where he could find the key. He won't say who told him. I have a good idea that it was you."

"Why would I do that?"

"That's my question."

Steve didn't answer.

"I can think of a very disturbing scenario. Suppose you met the Ellsworths out near their ranch. Suppose you were out so late Monday night that it turned into early Tuesday morning. You came across the Ellsworths stuck in the wash. One thing led to another and the Ellsworths were killed."

Steve was turning white. I removed my hand from his neck. He stayed in place. He was speechless.

I continued, "That could explain why you wanted Rodney to come up here. You knew what a klutz he is. If the house was vandalized and burglarized that would throw any investigation off. That would explain why you wanted the car messed up. Get rid off all the evidence. That would explain why you won't tell me why you want me to leave town. I threaten to expose you. Don't you see that by remaining silent, you become a prime suspect for murder?"

He was silent for a while. I gave him time to think.

I softened my voice. "You know that I am not the law. I have no authority to arrest you. I simply want to find my aunt and uncle. I love them. I'm concerned for their welfare. I have to understand your actions to get closer to the truth. Will you help me?"

Steve was silent for so long looking off in the corner that I thought I had lost. Then he turned and studied my face. I felt a glimmer of hope. He croaked, "Water."

I left him and stepped through the swinging door into the kitchen. I half feared that he would be gone when I got back with the cold water, but he was there.

He downed half the glass. "Tortillas make you thirsty," he said.

Then he turned and looked into the corner again. "You see that picture? The one with the Scouts? You see that kid next to Bishop Ellsworth? The one he has his arm around? That's me. That was one of the happiest days of my life."

"Go on," I said.

"I don't know what happened to the Ellsworths, and I'd tell you if I did. My part in this was because of a stupid piece of native copper. I have wished ever since that I could go back and change what I did, but what's done is too late." He looked down.

"You can go forward and strive to learn from your mistakes," I said.

He shook his head. "I had to one-up Lorenzo. He had found a small piece of native copper about the size of a Gatorade cap. I had to say, 'Is this all you have? It's nothing. Someone threw it away.' We argued about it, and then I had to tell him about the giant piece of native copper Bishop Ellsworth had. It was twenty pounds if it was an ounce. He showed it to us when we were working on our geology merit badge. That picture over there in the corner was taken after we passed it off. That was the only merit badge I ever completed."

Steve continued, "One thing led to another and basically to impress Suzie Parker I decided to borrow it from Bishop Ellsworth's office."

"How did you get the key?" I asked.

"I rang the doorbell to ask if I could borrow the native copper. When no one came I noticed the note to you taped to the door."

"What did it say?"

"I don't know. I just read far enough to realize I was too late. The Ellsworths were already gone. That's when I remembered the key. I saw Bishop Ellsworth stash it under that frog lawn ornament one time."

"And that same key fit the basement door? How did you find out?"

"I had Zam try it when we were thinking how to harass you. Anyway, I got the native copper and took it all over town and lost it. I lost it! Or someone took it. We all looked and we couldn't find it anywhere. There are none so blind as those who hid the native copper."

"So that's when you tried to cover it up?"

"Yeah. I messed up the office and then got Zam to come up and eat. He's a real pig. I knew he'd make a mess. I taped the key to the note so he could get in."

"Did you notice Bishop Ellsworth's computer or the piano?"

"Would they have been in the office? Wait, a piano is too big for the office."

"It's smaller than a regular piano. It's digital."

"I didn't notice either one, but the first time I was just looking for the native copper, and the second time I was just trying to mess things up."

"What about the Lexus?"

Steve looked away. "That was much later and we just happened across it."

"How did you know the road was even there? I was looking for it and would have missed the wheel tracks if Marco hadn't pointed them out."

"At the time we thought it was lucky. You probably noticed the beer cans. Well, we were tooling along having a good ole time when suddenly there were some headlights coming. You can go all night out there without meeting anyone, so we weren't prepared."

"For what?"

"The cops," Steve said, as if I had asked a dumb question. "We had all sorts of open containers. So we thought we were going off road to get out of sight. We hit that road by luck. It went over the hill like we wanted, so we followed it. Then when we came across the Lexus it seemed too good to pass up for the same reasons as I messed up the house."

"How much damage was there when you arrived?"

"Well, the window was busted and the steering column. I don't know if there was anything else."

"Why did you do more damage?"

"It wasn't just me!"

"You all."

"Things just got out of hand."

"The alcohol," I said.

Steve shrugged.

"Another thing. The first day I saw you in your pick-up pool there was no radio blaring. The second day, there was. I also noticed that the radio from the Lexus was stolen. There wouldn't be any connection between the two, would there?"

"Uh, I see your point."

"You need to make restitution."

"Resti...what?"

"Give it back."

"Consider it done."

"One other thing. You have made it your goal to get me to leave Ajo. That's not going to be easy. I told the Ellsworths I would housesit all summer. I made a commitment. I am bound by my promise to watch over this house. A few hardships won't be enough to make me turn tail and run."

"Sorry. It won't happen again."

"That's what you say when you're sober. Will it hold if you start drinking?"

"I see your point."

"That's what I thought."

At the door as he left, Steve paused. He looked back and said, "I learned one thing tonight. Confession is good for the soul."

"It's a step forward, but don't stop there," I said. "Confession only relieves the symptoms. It doesn't cure the disease. Now go straight home." I closed the door.

Why did I waste my breath with Steve? At his age, peers had much more influence over him than a teacher. I knew that any good intentions during our talk would vanish when he was back with his friends. He might even make another attempt to vandalize the cooler tonight.

I retrieved the mag light from the lawn, finding that it still worked. First I checked the basement door behind the palo verde. It was locked. Then I moved the tripwire for the alarm so that Steve would set it off before he got near its previous location.

Only then did I go back to bed in the hall bedroom. The laughter still rang through the guest room.

Chapter sixteen

I didn't get up until late the next day. I returned to the guest room where I had left everything heaped on the bed and the closet empty. All was now quiet.

I pulled out my cell phone and called Sandy. I said, "You Ajoites are sure night owls."

She said, "You didn't get any sleep, did you? What happened this time?"

"Not really very much, thanks to your suggestion about the alarm. Steve and company decided to help me choose to go back to California. They failed and instead I got the truth out of Steve. Most of it, anyway. Steve admits to using the key from under the ceramic frog to borrow a large piece of native copper. It was stolen from him, so the vandalism in the house was to cover up the loss of the copper. Same with the Lexus, which he says they came across by accident. But you can't use my evidence. I didn't use approved police methods to get him to talk."

"When the fingerprints get processed, we won't need your testimony."

"Did you know about the basement?"

"The boys helped stock it. Did they mess it up?"

"I'll find out when I get T.J. to open it. Rodney still has the key. I'll have those locks changed, too."

Sandy said, "I never thought about the basement when we were talking about locks. Bart never talks about it, so it slipped my mind."

I called T.J., who again seemed to be moving kind of slow. I took care of the watering and pool chores while waiting for him to arrive.

He came whistling from his truck, carrying his tool kit. I had no sooner showed him the door in the closet than it was open.

"It's a good thing I'm honest," he boomed. "I can generally open a door in less time than it takes me to find my keys."

He stood back to let me look in first. The door opened on a stairway heading down. "Are you game?" I asked.

He was. I flipped the light switch at the top of the stairs, finding the laugh box on the floor, just behind the door. I pocketed it. Thirteen steps down was another door, bigger and thicker than the one at the top. It was standing wide open with darkness beyond.

I flipped another light switch, and stepped into a huge storage room. It extended under most of the house, and it had strong beams and posts holding up the house above. It was filled with boxes, buckets, and barrels, all easily accessible, labeled and dated, containing wheat, oats, cornmeal, pinto beans, navy beans, pink beans, black beans, kidney beans, rice, potato pearls, dried milk, sugar, honey, shortening, textured vegetable protein, salt, and dried fruits and vegetables. There were shelves filled with home-canned fruits, vegetables, and meats. There were also paper products, soap, and barrels of water. Everything was in perfect order, as if stocked for an advertisement in a survivalist's magazine.

We walked around inspecting storage items as if we were touring a museum. Candles, oil lamps, lanterns, medical supplies, matches, batteries, cots, dishes, and cooking facilities were also stored there. Uncle Bart was ready to survive a nuclear holocaust.

The air was clean and fresh. The temperature was enough cooler than upstairs to make me wonder if I should move down here. A fleeting glimpse of a cricket scuttling behind a barrel and a scorpion stationary on the wall were the only vermin visible. The concrete floor was dust-free and there were no spider webs in the corners.

In one corner were several generators with fuel storage. Nearby was a desk with a computer and a pile of CD's. That piqued my interest.

The door on the far side was still locked, so it appeared Rodney hadn't come back.

I said, "Rodney Zamecki has the key. Could you change this lock, too?" For convenience, I had him change all three locks to match the ones he had already done. While T.J. worked, his hands operating without conscious direction, he asked about progress in finding the Ellsworths.

"Nothing yet. We know they haven't arrived at their usual camping spot or anywhere nearby. Thanks to Manny Molina, we have the license number and description of the RV that followed the green Lexus Tuesday morning, but we still haven't confirmed that there is any connection with their disappearance. It was rented in Denver, but we're still waiting for the rental information. We also have a picture of the driver, but so far nobody knows who he is. I got the story of the vandalism here and to the Lexus. There doesn't appear to be any connection with their disappearance."

"So some progress is being made. Speaking of missing persons, one time in Utah I stopped at a convenience store late at night. I had just finished a lock job. I noticed an elderly woman making a purchase, too well-dressed for that time and place. When I came out, she was just standing by her car. You know me. I struck up a conversation.

"She said she was going to Christmas dinner at her son's house in St. George. She said, 'If you could just direct me to the interstate, I can get there.' She seemed in full possession of her faculties and seemed believable.

"I said, 'Ma'am, you're more than a hundred miles from the interstate, and I think you missed your dinner.' It was after midnight, so it was already the twenty-sixth.

"Inquiring further, I discovered she had started at noon on a twenty-mile trip. I contacted the police, and sure enough she was missing. It turned out she went the wrong way on the freeway originally. She had met up with a police officer in another city and told him what she told me. He made sure she was headed in the right direction, but when the road narrowed she left the freeway and got lost. The police were able to contact her family to come get her so she wouldn't get lost again."

When T.J. finished the locks, he left. I went back to the basement and turned on the computer. I checked the pile of discs. Some of the discs had labels. Some were just given letters of the alphabet. Since none of the labels seeming promising, I started with "A." Bingo! It contained Uncle Bart's journal, the first one that was typed. "B" through "I" were successive years. There was no "J." Where was the back-up for the current year? I couldn't find it, and I didn't remember it from cleaning up the office. Could it have been wedged behind something? Or did it even exist? If Bart waited until the end of the year to do a back-up, I was sunk. Surely he would do it at least monthly, if not weekly or daily.

The doorbell was ringing when I came out through the closet. Marco was waiting.

"What kept you, Mr. White? I've been ringing the bell for ten minutes. My dad sent me up to see if you need any more help."

"Thanks, Marco."

"I think the javelinas trampled your flowerbed. Come take a look."

The plants below the hall bedroom window were mangled beyond resurrection. Stems were severed, blooms were shredded, leaves were already withered and dying. I had watered the east side that morning but hadn't taken a close look at the west.

Marco said, "What do you want done with these?" He had a bucket filled with black gravel.

"Where did you find that?" I asked.

"I got the bucket from the tool shed. The gravel was right there in the grass."

He pointed to an area adjacent to the flattened flower bed under the hall bedroom window.

Marco continued, "I noticed it when I was waiting for you to answer the door, so I picked up as much as I could. So it wouldn't be there when you mowed."

"Marco, you restore my faith in human nature. Let's

just toss it back in the parking area."

I poured the tiny gravel back in the parking area. "If you were going to simulate the sound of rain, how would you broadcast these on the roof?"

"Mr. Ellsworth has a hand crank seed spreader." Marco led the way to the tool shed, but the seed spreader was missing.

I wandered behind the shed to the hillside where the kids had disappeared when they ran from the alarm. Sure enough, the seed spreader, still with gravel in it, was ditched in the weeds.

After Marco left, I got through to Sandy. I told her about the back-up discs with computer. "If I can locate the current back-up disc, I may come up with more clues," I said. We discussed places it might be if it wasn't in the office. She told me about a junk drawer in the kitchen I hadn't come across and a shelf in the laundry room where odds and ends were placed.

Then Sandy invited me to choir practice at seven p.m. at the LDS Church. Remembering she was the choir director, I had no hesitation in committing to go. "It's for a special number in church tomorrow," she said, giving me directions. Fortunately, I already knew where the church was, not being good at following directions in unfamiliar territory.

The phone rang. A male voice asked for Bart Ellsworth.

"He's not here," I said. "May I take a message?"

"Tell him his truck is ready."

I couldn't believe my ears. "You mean the GMC?"

"Yes."

I said, "Bart is out of town right now, so it could be a few days before he picks it up. Can you tell me where the truck is?"

The truck was in Phoenix. Bart had taken it in several weeks ago to get the engine replaced. The company had promised him it would be done more than a week ago, but other jobs had taken longer than expected.

I immediately called Sandy with the information. She said, "That changes everything."

"Well, obviously they didn't go camping in the truck," I agreed. "I guess they went somewhere in the blue RV."

"It certainly looks like it, but just to cover all bases, some more checking will need to be done out at the ranch. I'll pull the Voluntary Independent Posse off searching for the note and send them to Ellsworth Ranch."

"I'd like to go, too," I said.

Sandy told me to wait an hour before going out so that she could get everything organized. "And don't leave home without your water."

I took a big drink of water and slipped my cell phone back in my pocket. I glanced at the time, pondering what to do until I could head out to the Ellsworth ranch.

The next thing I knew, I was waking up stiff and sore, and the time was 6:30. I had slept all afternoon. I couldn't believe I had missed helping search the ranch. I freshened up and headed down to choir practice, bringing a bottle of cold water with me.

The choir practice was in the sanctuary (they called it the chapel), not in a practice room like I was used to. The choir loft, unlike both churches in Greenwood City, was open to the view of the congregation. I liked being behind a partition when singing. Sandy and her organist were already there. One member of the bass section was seated, a man perhaps in his thirties with a calm, dignified, friendly manner. Sandy introduced him as Bishop

Reynolds. I sat down beside him, receiving a warm welcoming handshake. He immediately began asking questions about my aunt and uncle and what progress had been made in locating them. Then he delved into my own background, plans for the summer, and teaching experiences.

"You wouldn't also be the school principal, would you?" I asked.

Sandy called out, "I told you he'd catch on fast."

Bishop Reynolds laughed and continued the interview, seeking quite obviously to convince me to apply for the music job. Other members of the choir filtered it, all of them friendly and in good spirits. Everybody knew me before practice began and, except for Bishop Reynolds, I didn't remember a single name.

After the opening prayer, we got out the music for the anthem, except Sandy called it the "special number." Different church, different jargon. The choir was small, three basses, two tenors, three altos, five sopranos, but the blend and sound were good.

I noticed right away that the rules of this choir were different than mine. Talking, joking, and laughing were all permitted, while in my choirs such things were either discouraged or flatly prohibited. Sandy's choir was more fun than mine, but the music was mastered.

Sandy was a natural. She could hear anyone singing the wrong note and worked to fix the problems. Her approach of getting us to feel the music was far different than my nuts and bolts approach, but I began to see how I could use her techniques myself.

After practice, Bishop Reynolds told me straight out, "If you want the job, it's yours. Just fill out an application and send transcripts."

I was feeling good and said, "I just may do that. I'll come to the school Monday and pick up the form."

Sandy locked up, and we strolled out to the parking lot, where others were chatting before driving home.

Sandy told me that the Colorado plate Manny Molina saw had indeed crossed the Mexican border. On Monday it came into Arizona at Douglas. There was no record of it going into Mexico, either before or after. Also, the Denver police had come through with the rental information: David Bookbinder of Denver.

She said, "They interviewed neighbors since the Bookbinders are not home. They said that David and his wife left a week and a half ago for parts unknown. Apparently they just cruise around with no particular destination in mind each time they go on vacation, or at least no destination they are willing to divulge."

"Do they know Bart and Betty?"

"No one interviewed was able to say, but none of the contacts have any connection with Ajo, either."

I shook my head. "I can't fathom how someone could go off on vacation without a firm itinerary."

"I've done it," said Sandy, "but only when I was really depressed. Did you find the back-up disc?"

"No," I said wryly, admitting that I had slept instead.

"You must have needed it. You haven't slept through the night in Ajo yet, have you? The VIPs searched for Betty's note all morning, but found no trace of it. They got started at the ranch, but were planning to stop at dusk. They'll resume in the morning."

I said I would go out to help after church. Sandy reminded me to take water.

Sandy enquired if I had eaten, and when I admitted that I hadn't, she seemed very concerned. "I'll grab something when I get home," I promised.

We talked about the wildfires in Cochise County briefly. Sandy pointed out that June was the worst month for fires in Southern Arizona every year, due to the heat, low humidity, and almost total lack of rainfall.

Then she asked, "Are you really going to fill out the teaching application?"

"I don't know. I feel good enough about the situation to seriously consider it. But…."

"The jury is still out," finished Sandy. "That's understandable. You need to be certain before you make such a big change in your life."

Sandy sat in her car with the window down as we wrapped up our discussion. She turned the key. As the motor came to life, the radio switched on.

She turned it down, and then said, "Oh, I almost forgot to tell you, the radio that was stolen from the Lexus turned up. It was placed in front of the briefing room door with a note on it."

"Sounds like almost-restitution to me," I said.

I arranged to pick Sandy up for church in the morning, and I smiled all the way back to the hilltop. There I lost the smile.

At first it didn't seem too serious. The door of the tool room was wide open. I approached with caution, able to see by flashlight that it was empty. I closed the door and checked the yard. Coming around the fig tree, I smelled alcohol. Even more warily, I probed with my light.

I heard a noise by the swimming pool. I swung the mag light in that direction, pinning the proverbial deer with the bright light. It had foliage from the bushes hanging out the side of its mouth. The doe turned, leaped over McBain's fence in two bounds, and was gone.

A twig snapped behind me. I swung around, but could see nothing. Slowly I came to the east side of the house, the side toward the town. Nothing.

As I came near the orange tree, the branches suddenly shook and a flurry of beating wings sounded. I ducked down instinctively before I recognized that several roosting birds had erupted into the air.

I took a moment to settle my racing heart. I would have stopped looking at that point except for the brief smell of alcohol.

I looked at the base of the wall, hearing Debbie Piccioli practicing her flute. I continued around the house. When I got back to the tool shed the door was open, again.

Now I knew someone was here. Perhaps several some-ones. Was it Steve Paasch and his group, again? I hadn't heard any laughter, but I definitely needed to make sure the alarm was set before I went in.

Coming back to the fig tree, I smelled alcohol again. Where was it coming from? I swung my light back and forth. Nothing.

I probed deeper in the foliage, suddenly coming face to face with a snake. I could tell immediately that it wasn't venomous. It appeared to be some sort of whip snake, long and slender, a stripe running the length of its body. It slithered away from me quickly. I followed with my light, marveling how many seconds it took for its entire body to pass an open spot. Without pausing, it climbed the citrus tree. It went right up the branches. Every once in a while it stopped, becoming the exact image of the branches themselves. That it could climb so quickly and confidently scared me. How could I be comfortable around trees, especially after dark?

The shed door suddenly slammed. I pointed the mag light and ran toward the noise even as I realized I should be more cautious. Before I could slow down, something crashed into my skull, and I was out cold.

Chapter seventeen

My head felt pulverized. Smell returned—Bermuda grass; then hearing—birds chirping. What a cliché. My arms itched. Bermuda always made me itch. My mouth was dried out, swollen. I turned my head without making the throbbing any worse, a good sign, I thought. Slowly I got up and checked the house. The doors were secure. Inside, nothing had been touched. So I was the target.

I went back out, looked around and found a shovel leaning against the pool wall. It hadn't been there yesterday. It had been in the tool room. I remembered the open door. Could I have been hit with the flat part of the shovel? I found a small amount of blackened blood and some brown hairs.

I very seldom got headaches, and the pain was beginning to ebb. I took a couple of ibuprofen pills to hasten the process and took a long soaking bath. In the end I looked okay in my light blue shirt and tie and navy blue slacks. I had brought a matching suit coat, but didn't even consider wearing it. My carefully combed hair didn't show the knot, but it was quite tender to the touch. I took too long. I had no time for breakfast if I was to pick up Sandy. I would eat as soon as church was over. I gulped several glasses of water.

I arrived in front of Sandy's home about five minutes early, but she came out immediately. She wore a red and white dress which complemented her tan complexion. Her dimple disappeared when I told her what had happened to me.

"So the only thing you sensed was the smell of alcohol?" she asked. "I can try to take prints off the shovel, I suppose."

"I picked it up when I checked for blood," I admitted.

"Maybe we'll get lucky. Before bed last night I tried the name David Bookbinder on everyone I could reach. No one recognized it. Maybe someone at church…"

The name was on the tip of her tongue as we entered the foyer. Many people greeted her, no doubt drawn by an unfamiliar male companion. If she didn't mind the speculation in everyone's eyes, I wouldn't mind either. She asked everyone if they knew Bookbinder, but no one did. I was welcomed so much I thought my hand would cramp up.

Sacrament meeting, for which the choir was to sing, was first. I sat in the bass section just behind Sandy. She wore subtle perfume. We sang three hymns for prelude, and as good as Sandy was at directing in practice, she was even better with an audience. She was a ball of fire, directing with joyful intensity, using her whole body to get the choir to follow, sing from the heart, and genuinely enjoy themselves.

The first speaker had hardly begun when I heard a cell phone on vibrate. Sandy quickly shut it off, glanced at me, aware I had heard it, and walked out of the chapel to speak. Several minutes later she returned to the door, beckoned to me, and I joined her.

She reminded me that the VIPs had been continuing their search of the Ellsworth Ranch. "I need to leave, and I wanted you to know why."

"What did they find?" I asked quietly. She hesitated, and my mouth went dry. I repeated, "What did they find?"

She chose her words carefully, willing me to understand and not worry. "It has obviously been out in the sun for a long time. Weeks, at the very least, probably months. It isn't recent." Still she hesitated, but then told me, "It's a human skull."

Sandy tried in vain to get me to stay for the rest of the meetings, but she needed a ride and my attention was suddenly elsewhere. She got one of the altos to lead the music for the rest of the service. I dropped her at her house so that she could change. I offered to be her chauffeur, accepted no for an answer, and drove back to the Ellsworth house.

As I came to a stop on the black gravel I thought of Shibasaburo Takamine. Would he recognize the name of David Bookbinder? I went next door before I changed. Cal Pinegar was sitting with Shibasaburo. Cal said Gladys was playing the organ in her church.

I asked Shibasaburo if he recognized the name of David Bookbinder. He held my hands in his and screwed his head around so that his wild eyes, peering sideways, gazed directly at me. He shook his head.

Back home, I changed clothes, noticing that the trumpet was missing again. Knowing I needed to eat even though I wasn't hungry, I looked in the refrigerator. I found some ham and cheese in the meat drawer. I wondered if it had spoiled when the refrigerator door was left ajar, but as I picked up the ham, my hand froze. I couldn't believe my eyes. Underneath, in a plastic bag, was a back-up disc. It was labeled with the letter "J."

Hurriedly putting the food back, I almost ran to the basement. I inserted the disc in the computer with trembling hands. It was the back-up to Bart's missing journal. I went immediately to the last entry, which was Monday.

Packed. Eddy on Stone line: colonies!

'Packed,' I understood, but who was Eddy? What was the Stone line? Was Eddy riding a bus or train to the colonies? What colonies? Wait a minute! My mother's maiden name was Stone, as was my Aunt Betty's. Could George Ellsworth have been correct about this disappearance relating to family history?

I went through the rest of the journal, starting January 1, skimming a lot, looking for key words. In January:

Talked to Bookbinder about genealogy problems. He suggested Eddy. Will call.

I assumed this was David Bookbinder, but who was Eddy? The next day:

Eddy agreed to help on Stone line. Part time. We need professional help.

I remembered the file filled with family trees. Genealogy was the key. In February:

Temple: great session. Completed ordinances for Ellsworth line back to 1187! Stones are next.

In early April:

Betty invited Ted to house sit this summer. Accepted! Shocked not only that he accepted, but that he gave his answer so readily. Out of character. His breakup with Janet must have really hurt him, but now we can travel without worries.

Later in April:

Eddy found Stone connection in St. George. Polygamy. Genealogist's nightmare!

I found nothing else with the name David Bookbinder and no more mentions of Eddy, whoever he was, until the last entry. Instead of clearing things up, the journal complicated matters. Perhaps Sandy could understand more than I did from these cryptic passages. Ejecting the disc, I put it in my shirt pocket and went up through the closet.

As I started filling my canteen, my cell phone rang. Ellen Kramer said, "We're leaving Payson on the way to Ajo. Anything new there?"

"I finally found the CD with your dad's journal on it. He consulted with a guy named Bookbinder and another guy named Eddy. He makes reference to the Stone line, polygamy, and the colonies."

"Of course!" Ellen said. "Dad and Mom just finished the Ellsworth line back to something like the 12th century. They have been stuck for ages on Mom's side. The LDS colonies were in Northern Mexico. When U.S. laws changed, polygamists took refuge there."

"Bookbinder's RV came through Douglas from Mexico on Monday," I said.

"They must have gotten a lead and couldn't wait," said Ellen, "but my mother just wouldn't leave without letting you know."

"I've confirmed she left a note," I said, "but it got lost. She probably told Gladys Takamine, but she doesn't remember. My cell phone was inadvertently turned off."

Ellen said, "I checked with some friends in the

Springerville/Eager area. My parents haven't shown up for church there. If they come this afternoon my friends will call. Scott is on his way to Ajo too. He was leaving Flagstaff a few minutes ago. See you when we get there."

I finished filling my canteen, also took a gallon bottle of water, and drove to Ellsworth Ranch. I wanted to let Sandy know what I had found.

A VIP member posted at the turnoff to the ranch caused me to drive on by and not attempt the direct approach. Around the bend I parked under a mesquite tree in the arroyo and decided to walk in. I paused to slather on sunscreen, put on my hat, and check my belt pouch for binoculars. Often I carried energy bars in it, but I had removed them because of the heat.

Hiking in the shade of the trees lining the arroyo, I felt my usual exhilaration when out in nature. The heat didn't seem to bother me as much as before, even though there was no wind and the temperature soared. I wondered if it had reached the predicted 120°F, air temperature, not full sun temperature.

When I got close to Ellsworth Ranch, I could see that all the action was up the side canyon, the idyllic hole in the rock with the dripping spring. I climbed over rocks, around palo verde, and through dense stands of cholla cactus on my way up the slope to the rim of the side canyon. My body protested, not used to such exertion in the heat, but frequent stops to sip from my water jug helped me keep my wind.

The opportunities for shade were fewer the higher I got until there was no shade at all, just granite as hot as lava rocks in a kiln. Following the ridge to the box canyon, I found the scene of the investigation. I splashed water on the spot where I intended to sit to cool it somewhat, then wet my shirt, neck and face with the remaining water in the gallon jug. I still had plenty of water in my trusty canteen.

I drew out my binoculars and settled down to watch. As I focused on Sandy, she turned and looked up at me. I held up the back-up disc and signed that I needed to talk to her when she was done. She nodded and bent to her work.

I noted five triangular flags placed around the amphitheater. It appeared that body parts, or probably bones or clothing, had been discovered scattered around. I was too far above and my field glasses too weak to make out much.

A number of other officers were there, including Deputy Mendez. Sandy took photographs, collected evidence, and made notes. After forty-five minutes to an hour, I got a terrible cramp. I almost fell from my perch, massaging the knotted muscle in my calf.

Eventually the evidence was removed from the scene in body bags, and Sandy directed me by gestures to meet her at the mouth of the side canyon. I nodded and set about getting down safely. The ascent was always easier than descent. Rubble and cactus were intermixed and the slope was steep and the sun beat down. My body felt stiff and sore, and my calf knotted up twice more. I felt lightheaded, almost wobbly, and my head began to ache.

Sandy beat me to the main arroyo, and I could see her following my progress, paralleling me. If she hadn't been waiting for me, I might have taken a longer, safer route, but I hated to delay her. At the top of a sharp slope, thirty feet above the sand, I decided to take a short cut. I drained the last of my canteen and inched my way down, testing each foothold before committing to it. The sun beat into my back and the heat radiated from the rocks before me. More than halfway down that last stretch, doing well, I felt dizzy. I lost track of where I was and almost fell, managing to cling to the rocks more by luck than anything else.

Sandy's voice came through the haze in my head. "Ted, are you all right?"

"Fine," I grunted, fighting to hang on and clear my head.

"What's wrong?"

"Nothing." By this time my head had cleared, and I made it safely down.

I turned to talk to Sandy, suddenly dizzy again, falling, blackness closing in swiftly. I was out before I hit the sand.

Chapter eighteen

Smell returned first—the institutional smell of a hospital. Then hearing: a distant intercom paging a doctor. I was cold except for my hand. My mouth was dry, but not swollen. Finally, I opened my eyes. My first sight was of Sandy, head bowed, eyes puffy, makeup smudged. Her eyes closed, she hadn't noticed I was awake. Since she was holding my hand, I squeezed gently.

That galvanized her into joy. "You're awake! Nurse, he's awake!"

I said to Sandy, "What happened? I remember being dizzier than I've ever felt before and I remember falling. I don't remember landing."

"You fainted, and I couldn't wake you. How do you feel?"

"I've felt better," I said.

"We called an ambulance but the crew was unable to revive you. You got a medical helicopter ride here, and you've been in a coma ever since."

"How long…?"

"Twenty-four hours. Almost twenty-five."

I couldn't believe it. "Have my aunt and uncle made

contact yet? Any progress?"

Sandy shook her head.

"Where is 'here'?"

"Desert Sky Medical Center in Phoenix."

"Where is that in relation to Ajo?"

"A hundred miles north."

A doctor ambled in, introducing himself as Dr. Dixon.

I told him about getting dizzy while descending the last steep slope. "So, what got me? Heat stroke? And I thought I was keeping hydrated."

Dr. Dixon frowned. "How much water did you drink?"

"I don't even know, I drank so much. I couldn't seem to quench my thirst. I drank almost six quarts on my hike alone."

"What had you eaten?"

I couldn't remember. I finally worked out that I hadn't eaten much of anything since Friday night in the Copper Cafe. I felt extremely weak and sick, and my head ached.

Dr. Dixon said a number of tests had been done. Not all of them had been completed, so he couldn't definitively say what had afflicted me. However, he believed that the root cause was electrolyte depletion. "When you don't eat right and drink a lot of water, you lose electrolytes. I've suspected this might be the problem since you were first brought in. I've been giving you electrolytes in your IV."

"Are you saying I may have drunk too much water?"

"Coupled with not eating properly. It's dangerous, but since you have come out of the coma, I would expect a full recovery. I'll know more when all the tests come back, of course."

"Uh, what exactly are electrolytes?"

"Substances whose molecules dissociate into their constituent ions when they're dissolved."

Seeing my uncomprehending expression, he went on in plainer English. "Take sodium. Your body needs the sodium ions to regulate the body's water balance. When you perspire a lot, you flush the ions out of your system. Then all sorts of things start to go wrong. I'll bet you had a pretty bad cramp on your little hike. You probably got tired more quickly than usual and were unusually weak. The dizzy spell you told me about is a classic symptom."

"I just thought it was the heat."

"At the end, your blood pressure dropped so suddenly you were thrown into a coma. We're seeing more and more of this as people do strenuous exercise in the heat and don't eat."

"What about the blow to his head I told you about?" asked Sandy. "Did that make his condition worse?"

"It's possible, but I doubt it. There's no fracture." After a thorough exam, Dr. Dixon said it was unlikely that I had a concussion.

I asked how soon I would be released.

He said, "Not today. We'll see how you do before we make any plans. Let's see if we can get you out of the ICU first." He stopped at the door. "We have a gentleman who's been living in an RV out in the parking lot and haunting the halls all day waiting for you to wake up. He claims to be your next of kin. Do you feel up to a visit? No more than five minutes."

I wondered who it could be. My stepfather was in Pennsylvania and my uncle was missing. Was it Scott? I turned to Sandy. "How do you get to stay if he only gets five minutes? Not that I mind."

"I just act like I belong," she said. "I followed the ambulance in my car to the landing zone in Gila Bend. There was no room in the helicopter, so I drove to the hospital. You were already in intensive care when I got here."

Just then a huge black man wearing a ridiculously small hospital gown strode into the room. "What d'you mean, scaring us half to death?" T.J. said.

"Next of kin?" I questioned.

"We're brothers! Speaking of kin, is there anyone you would like me to contact to let them know where you are?"

"There are three people I should tell, but two are missing. I guess I should tell my mom, but I'll wait until I've been released. There's nothing she can do, and I don't want her to worry."

"That's a pretty selfish attitude," said T.J. "What if she wants to come be by your side? What if she wants to pray for you? Give her a chance!"

He made sense, sort of, but I couldn't remember her phone number. Learning that my belt pouch and wallet were in a drawer, I told him where the number was. "Lorraine Hudson. She's remarried."

I faded in and out of sleep for the next several hours. Whenever I awoke, Sandy was right beside me.

Early in the evening I was moved out of the ICU and rolled in the bed to a regular room. I was put on a liquid diet with the promise of real food the next day if I continued to improve. T.J. came in as I was finishing my Jell-O. Sandy was out of the room at the time.

I said, "T.J., why are you hanging around? Don't you have anything better to do?"

"I'm your ride home. Last I checked, your truck

wasn't in the parking lot, and Sandy will have to leave tonight to go back to work in the morning."

"I hadn't even thought about my truck," I said. "I guess it's still in the arroyo where I parked it."

"Or else Border Patrol has had it towed," laughed T.J.

"Still," I said, "you're in Phoenix, the big city, a hundred miles from Ajo. Live it up! At least go see a movie."

"I don't remember the last time I was even tempted."

"There have to be bookstores in the area."

"I'm in the middle of a good, old-fashioned mystery."

"Go see a ball game."

"The Arizona Diamondbacks? I don't think so. I'm a Dodger fan from way back. Besides, I came here on a job."

"What job?"

"Messenger boy. I reached your mother. She sends her love and wants you to call as soon as you're able. She wants you to know she will be praying for you, and she asked me to look after you. She can't come because she's recovering from heart bypass surgery. She said there was nothing you could do, and she didn't want you to worry, so she didn't tell you. She's home now."

"She what?" I heard myself and smiled. "At least you know how I come by my attitudes."

"Also, I was talking to one of the paramedics that transported you." T.J. lowered his voice. "When you fainted, Sandy radioed for an ambulance, but it took awhile for them to get out to the ranch. Sandy administered CPR. Your heart and breathing had both stopped, but she kept you alive. Then your heart started again, and you started breathing on your own, but you still weren't responsive. The paramedic told me Sandy was really worried that she hadn't done CPR correctly and that she had caused the coma."

"She saved my life," I said. "It really brings home… how close…a call…"

I dozed off again. When I awoke, Sandy was seated beside me. I said, "I heard a rumor that someone in this room saved my life."

Sandy said, "If I were you, I wouldn't give any credence to whatever rumor you've heard."

I said, "If that person is in this room, I would sure like to show my gratitude." I looked straight into her eyes.

She couldn't hold my gaze. She bowed her head, twisted her hands, and said, "I have a confession to make. I had never done CPR on a real person before. When you started breathing again I was so relieved, but then you didn't wake up. I was sure it was my fault. God heard my prayers. So thank Him, not me."

"Okay, I will, and I think I'm improving. Something just occurred to me that should have been foremost on my mind when I woke up. I came across Uncle Bart's back-up disc in the meat drawer of the refrigerator right before I came out to the ranch. No wonder I couldn't find it. He wrote about Bookbinder with no first name and Eddy with no last name. He mentioned the Stone line, polygamy, and colonies. Ellen thinks the Stone family went to the colonies in Mexico when the United States prohibited polygamy."

"At last a solid lead. I agree with Ellen. This will enable us to find them. And I wanted to tell you that the bones in the hole in the rock have been there for years. Decades. They're really old."

"Good," I said, even as I faded back to sleep.

Sandy was dozing in the chair beside me when I awoke. I studied her smooth face—full of vitality when awake, and serene as she slept. Her lips turned up at the corners in a permanent smile, but her dimple came and went.

I knew I had found a friend for life in Mrs. Blanca Alicia Sandino, aka Detective Sandy Sandino, but I began to worry. Sandy was a married woman.

I faded back to sleep.

Chapter nineteen

Sandy was looking at me when I woke up in the hospital room, the dimple in her left cheek suddenly appearing. "Wow," I said, "we're both awake at the same time. Are you rested enough to drive back to Ajo?"

"Oh, yes. That won't be a problem, if I can ever get started." She made no move to stand up.

Remembering my summer job, I asked, "Is anything being done to keep the Ellsworth's yard watered?"

"Manny Molina has added it to his list. When I asked him, he told me he already has a key should he need to get in. He borrowed it from Gladys Takamine several weeks ago when your aunt and uncle were gone for a few days. He forgot to give it back."

"That explains how he could enter so quietly in the dark," I said, telling Sandy about the trumpet disappearing and reappearing. "Now wait just a minute," I said. "I had the locks changed. How did the old key help?"

"Manny is a man of many talents," said Sandy. "Perhaps he has learned a thing or two about locks from T.J."

"Maybe," I said doubtfully. "So now that you know

more or less where the Ellsworths are, how do we go about finding them?"

"First I need to do a little research. There were a number of colonies in the Mexican states of Sonora and Chihuahua. Surely someone I can reach will know which colony the Stone family lived in."

"Something else bothers me," I said. I hesitated.

"The UDA danger?" prompted Sandy.

"Exactly. We don't know if Betty and Bart ever reached the colony. What if they were waylaid out at the ranch?"

"Border Patrol ruled out—"

"Not the ones who stole the car. What if someone was there when they parked? The blue RV could hold a lot of UDAs. Where did it vanish to?"

"I've been assuming it took Betty and Bart to the colony."

"The RV didn't go back to Mexico. You said Customs only showed it coming into the U.S."

"I don't think they get all outbound vehicles recorded, but I see your point. I still think it's unlikely that another group of UDAs were involved."

"Unfortunately, the unlikely has been happening. Who would have thought Steve Paasch would have broken into the house almost as soon as Betty and Bart left? And Rodney Zamecki. Twice. And the attack on the cooler. Twice."

Sandy's eyes flashed. "And the attack on you. We need to make an arrest before that happens again."

"That would be nice," I said.

"That's why I have to go back to work. Others have examined the scene and they think they know who attacked you."

"Who was it?"

"I can't tell you. I need to review their findings before we act on it. If we make an arrest, I'll tell you."

"Do I get a victim's rights card?"

"I'll tell you personally."

I chuckled, enjoying talking to Sandy. "Is T.J. hanging around the hospital as a bodyguard? Do you fear another attempt?"

"No, he's hanging around because he's your friend. That's what friends do."

"I barely know him."

"We had a long time to talk while we waited for you to rejoin the world. You listen to him. He finds that remarkable. And it isn't just surface attention. You listen to all the nuances. I've noticed that, too."

"Steve asked how I got to be friends with everyone in town so fast."

Sandy laughed musically.

I continued, "What could I tell him? You people have befriended me. And after the last few months in Greenwood City…"

Sandy said, "That bad, huh?"

"You guys have restored my faith in people."

"Well, if you're going to get all mushy, I'd better be on my way." Sandy remained seated. Then her dimple disappeared. "I know where you're coming from. When my husband died I was an emotional basket case. If it hadn't been for friends like Bart and Betty, I wouldn't have made it." Sandy fell silent, a pensive furrowing of her brow marring her smooth skin.

'So she's a widow,' I thought.

Sandy stood, ready to go. She paused in the doorway, fixing an eye on me. "Don't think you can get away with forgetting your promise just because you were in a coma and in the hospital."

"What did I forget?" I asked, mystified.

"You see?" she said impishly. "Pretending won't get you off the hook. Don't you remember promising to pick up an application to teach?"

"I haven't forgotten."

"A likely story. The first thing you did after making the promise was get hit in the head by a shovel, and the second thing was fall off a mountain."

"Fall?" I disputed playfully. "Never!"

"Just remember the first thing you have to do when you get back to Ajo is go to the school."

"Yes, Ma'am," I said in mock sincerity.

Sandy laughed lightheartedly and left. I faded back to sleep. But my slumber didn't last. It was a rough night. I wasn't able to stay awake or asleep, and the nurses weren't as good of company as Sandy. I worried that I was getting too close to Sandy when I needed some space. Then I worried that she might be getting too close to me, and I would hurt her by wanting some space.

By six a.m. I was pretty well awake, and feeling almost like it might be possible to get back to normal, maybe. According to the TV, all the fires in Cochise County were now under control except one, but not the one I expected. The Naco fire straddling the Mexican border had suddenly jumped the fire lines and gotten away, again. It didn't help that there was a communication problem between the U.S. and Mexican firefighters. Even though the Bear Hollow fire was no longer a problem, the footage shown five times during the fire coverage was of the pine tree being engulfed that had excited Marco. The footage was misleading when the coverage dealt with the containment of the fires, but it was unquestionably impressive.

After eating real food for breakfast, I dug out my cell phone. No sooner had I placed the phone on the bedside table than it rang.

"Good morning," I said, thinking it was Sandy.

A baritone voice said, "Did I get the right number? Aren't you supposed to be hospitalized?"

It was my Greenwood City principal, Dr. Becker.

I said, "How did you find out?"

"What is some podunk principal doing tampering with my award-winning band director?"

"I haven't—"

"Good, and make sure you don't. I'm the one who molded you into the band director you are. Don't you think you owe a little loyalty to me and to Greenwood City? Without all of us, you wouldn't have won any state titles."

"I'm sure the principal here was just calling to advise—"

"I don't buy that for an instant. He's trying to steal you away. I don't know where this Reynoso character is coming from, but he's got a fight on his hands."

"Reynolds."

"How much money is he offering? There's no way he can match what we're giving you. Hey Joe High School? I can't even Google it. What's his offer?"

"We haven't even—"

"And you better not. Did you know that the school board has authorized a stipend for making it to state competition in all sports and activities, including band and orchestra? It was passed Thursday. Retroactive to this last school year. It should be direct deposited next week. A nice tidy sum. And with your record, it should be a gimme each year."

"I hadn't heard—"

"It was hush-hush. A reward for a job well done. And think of all the band students you would be letting down if you moved away. One of the reasons they join is because of the success the band has had since you took over. What kind of a band would you have down there? They have more saguaros than students. You'd have no way of challenging the big schools in Tucson and Phoenix. Here you've made it to the top. All you have to do is keep doing what you're doing."

"I—"

"And another thing. You like to go hiking. You never got so much as a scratch up here. Down there, first time out, hospital. Cactus and thorns and heat and fangs. Forget it. Come back home where it's safe."

"Earthquakes—"

"When was the last one? I mean that you really felt? Take my word for it. You'd be much better off in Greenwood City. You've made it to the top. Reap the benefits. Whadayou say?"

"I don't know."

"Course you do. You'll see. Soon as you feel better you'll see. Hey, good talking to you. Drop by when you get back."

Dr. Becker disconnected. I felt as dizzy as usual when he talked to me. He was right about the community support and my salary. I was sure Ajo couldn't match those. But then, the cost of living in Ajo was much lower, too.

I put no stock in Dr. Becker's assertion that he made me, and his assumption that he could buy me turned me off, too.

I had only spoken to Bishop Reynolds once, but he had already gained my respect. He had integrity. Dr. Becker's call only served to remind me how much I disliked the man.

Dr. Dixon, frown firmly in place, came by for a few minutes to let me know that his diagnosis of electrolyte depletion had been confirmed by all the tests. He said if I continued to progress, I would be discharged tomorrow. He told me to begin walking.

After Dr. Dixon left, T.J. sauntered in and helped me up. He pushed the IV stand and walked at my slow pace one circuit around the nurses' station in the middle of the pod. I couldn't believe how weak I was. Sunday I had thought nothing of climbing a mountain. However, I could feel strength returning.

When I was settled back in bed, T.J. suggested I sleep some more, but I was wide awake. I didn't see how I could have slept so much yesterday. T.J. had barely started one of his patented stories when a voice said, "Knock! Knock! Anybody home?"

Bishop Reynolds came in, bringing his own brand of energy. T.J. excused himself.

I said, "Dr. Becker called just a few minutes ago."

Bishop Reynolds said, "Good. I was hoping he would be concerned about you."

"Actually, he accused you of tampering."

He stared at me as if he couldn't believe what I had said. "I'm sorry to have put you in such an uncomfortable position. I guess I let it slip that I was hoping to get you to come to Ajo, but surely it's your decision, not his. You're not under contract for next year, are you?"

"No. And it is my decision to make. I just haven't made it."

"Then I'm sure you'll make a wise one. I'm going to a job fair at Arizona State University in a few minutes. I'll let you know if you have any competition. So far we haven't found anyone willing to come to Ajo. Since you couldn't come to the school today and I was going right past, I brought the teaching application we talked about. I can leave it or not, as you choose."

"Thank you," I said. "Sandy made me promise to pick it up as soon as I get back to town."

He laid it on my bedside table.

My cell phone rang as Bishop Reynolds headed for the door. As he left, I answered on the last ring.

It was Sandy. After quizzing me on my progress, she said, "Both Ellen and Scott made it to Ajo."

"Ironic," I said. "The changing of the guard."

"They're staying in a motel. Thanks to you, their keys don't work," said Sandy. "Wish me luck. I'm about to make an arrest in the case of the assault of a potential band director for Ajo High School."

I did two laps around the pod with the help of a nurse, but no faster than the first time. I was back in bed, beginning to get drowsy, when there was a tap on the door frame. I looked up to find a grim Manny Molina coming in with Maria Tirado, the tortilla lady. Manny had my trumpet case.

Manny said in his breathy voice, "We heard you were getting better."

We discussed electrolyte depletion, a topic Manny was interested in due to his outdoor work. He gave me some practical advice on avoiding it in the future.

Maria thanked me for letting her know how well Manny played the trumpet. She said, "I found him working at the Plaza and introduced myself."

I said, "Didn't you know him before that?"

Maria flushed. "I knew who he was, but we had never met."

Manny looked at me. "She talked me into at least trying to play again. I said I had no trumpet."

"I told him to buy one," said Maria.

"No one in Ajo sells trumpets," said Manny. "Then I remembered the key I borrowed from Gladys Takamine."

"Why didn't you just ask to borrow my trumpet?" I asked.

"It was too late that night. The house was dark. I had to work the early shift Saturday. You had already said I could borrow it any time."

"I'll bet you were shocked when your key didn't work," I said. "I had T.J. Tatum change the locks."

Manny started laughing. "That's why it didn't turn. I thought I brought the wrong key. But then I cheated. Right after T.J. got to Ajo, I had to get him to open a locked shed. The key had been lost. I was amazed how quickly he opened it. I got him to teach me. I used what he taught me to get through his own lock job."

"I knew it was you Friday night," I said. "The pesticide smell preceded you. Did you borrow the trumpet again Sunday morning?"

"Right after you went to church. And again Sunday night. I didn't know you were in the hospital until yesterday. Once I started playing it all came back. To be able to hear again by watching Maria's face…" He couldn't express his feelings in words. He continued, "Don't judge harshly. I'm only a beginner. I will improve. How can I ever thank you?"

Manny reverently unpacked my trumpet, warmed up briefly, and then softly played a song for me. He looked at Maria as he played, her face glowing in the warmth of the music. He played as beautifully as Gladys Takamine said. I could see what he meant about a face being elastic and expressive. It was a simple love song. Maria's love for him leaped out of every movement of her face. It was hard to tell if the music put the love in Maria's face or if her love drew out the music. It was enchanting to listen and watch.

When Manny finished I said, gesturing to the trumpet, "It's yours. I can't produce tones like that. I would deem it an honor to get you outfitted for the community band."

"Now, wait," said Manny. "I can't accept—" Maria put her hand over his mouth, silencing him, and stopped him from handing me the trumpet.

"He means, 'Thank you,'" she said simply.

Manny turned angrily to Maria, "But what will *he* do for a trumpet? It's his instrument."

I said, "I have a clarinet and a flute with me. My best trumpet is still in California."

Manny didn't get the message because he was still looking at Maria, so she repeated, "His best trumpet is still in California. Now be gracious and thank him."

Manny threw up his hands in surrender. He turned to me. "See how bossy Maria is? This is how I got talked into trying the trumpet, again. Thank you," he growled, and then he winked at me.

I thanked Manny for helping water the plants at the Ellsworth's.

He said, "Maria helped."

Maria said, "I watered this morning. What happened to the flower bed on the west side by the house?"

"It's a long story," I said.

As Manny and Maria left hand in hand, they were approached by a nurse who asked if they could bring such beautiful music to other patients. Manny nodded, and Maria glowed with pleasure.

I did some more walking. After three times around the nurses' station, I was ready for a nap.

A familiar laugh, quickly stifled, woke me from my snooze. Scraggly red beard, freckles, red hair. Steve Paasch was peeking around the privacy curtain. T.J. Tatum was nowhere in sight. Perspiration broke out on my brow.

Chapter twenty

I blinked. The head wasn't there. I didn't hear a sound. The curtain was still. Had I been dreaming? If it was a dream, the only part I remembered was the aborted laugh and Steve Paasch's head.

Just as I picked up my cell phone, T.J. stepped into the room.

"I was just going to call you," I said.

"Are you okay? I just saw Steve going down the hall."

"So I wasn't dreaming," I said. "How do you know him?"

"You're the Johnny-come-lately to Ajo, not me. I set up shop on Main Street Ajo. Who drives by forty-leven times a day? He stops to talk from time to time."

T.J. settled into the chair.

I said, "Do you suppose Steve is the one who clobbered me with the shovel? Sandy could be looking for him to arrest right now, and he's up here."

"If he really wanted to harm you, he had some opportunities he passed up. I think he's getting a bad rap."

"But he admitted to burglary and vandalism."

"At worst it seems to me he's guilty of malicious mischief."

"Did you see the Lexus?"

"I've seen worse, and that was with a mob mentality. Trashing the office is more his style."

"He also admits," I yawned hugely, "to underage consuming."

T.J. quieted and allowed me to drop off to sleep. When I awoke, Marco was in T.J.'s chair.

I said, "Marco, thank you for coming."

Marco didn't look up. He had the earbuds in again. I reached out and touched his arm.

Marco hastily removed the MP3 connectors. "My dad came with me, but you were asleep. He went to visit Steve's grandfather."

"Am I ever going to meet…. Did you say 'Steve's grandfather?'"

"Yeah. I don't know what's wrong with him, but he's here a lot."

"So is Steve here with him?"

"I think so. He came up with his grandmother on Saturday evening. I'll bet they stayed over."

"Do you know when they left Ajo?"

"Let's see. I was pumping up my tire…"

"Again?"

"It keeps getting soft, but I can't find a leak. I think it was around seven. They stopped to fill up their rusty ole station wagon."

Marco's cell phone rang. He listened a moment and then said, "Okay, be right there."

Pocketing his cell phone, he said. "Sorry, gotta run. My dad is ready to go. Just one more thing. Have you made any progress in finding the Ellsworths?"

"We think they went to an old Mormon colony south of Douglas to locate some lost genealogy records. We're going tomorrow to find them."

"You're getting out?" Marco broke into a smile.

"That's the plan."

"That's great! Bye!"

Then it hit me. If Steve was leaving town at the beginning of choir practice Saturday night, he couldn't have wielded the shovel after practice. It wasn't him.

I struggled out of the hospital bed and did some more walking. T.J. found me on the far side of the nurses' station.

He said, "Any improvement?"

"A little," I exaggerated. "Steve was on the way here when I was assaulted, by the way. It wasn't him."

"Told ya so," said T.J.

Sandy called asking about my progress.

"I'm ready to climb another mountain," I lied.

Sandy continued, "Ellen and Scott found a map of the Mormon colonies in Northern Mexico online. They left messages for people who should know which one the Stones lived in. I expect to find out this evening which one it was."

Bishop Reynolds dropped by on his way back to Ajo. He had signed one new teacher, but the others who interviewed were looking at Ajo as a last resort. He was sure they would go elsewhere. No one interviewed for the music opening.

As Bishop Reynolds trudged out the open door, I was tempted to call him back to brighten his day by accepting the job. 'No,' I admonished myself, 'wait until you're sure.'

I was pretty sure now that I needed to leave Greenwood City, but was Ajo really a better place?

I was still gazing out the open door where Bishop Reynolds had vanished when a redhead slouched by on the far side of the hall. He turned just as he left my field of vision and I saw the scraggly beard. Steve Paasch.

The red hair reappeared right at the doorway. Steve looked in first, then scanned up and down the corridor. He entered, his hand still in his pocket.

I said, "Steve, good to see you. You're a long ways from home."

He came over to the bed. He stood there. He didn't come around to the chair as most people did.

He said, "So, California Guy, why are you here?"

"Electrolyte depletion."

"Elec—?"

"The heat got me. Didn't you know? Isn't that why you came?"

"No, I've been trapped here with my grandfather all weekend and my grandmother conflagrated my cell phone. How did it happen?"

"I went on a short hike Sunday. I drank too much water without eating properly and fainted."

"Does that mean you're going back to California?"

"Is that your hope?"

"Not really. You'd be better than Wilcox."

"What changed your mind?"

"You didn't call the cops. You listened." He shrugged. "Nobody listens to teenagers."

"I hope your grandfather gets better."

"He's got the big C."

"My dad had cancer."

"He died, right?"

"They can do a lot more now."
"Yeah, right."
"You'll see."
"Anyway," said Steve, "I brought you something."

Chapter twenty-one

Steve handed me a figurine about four inches tall of a saguaro set in an ancient Indian pot. The words "Welcome to Arizona" were printed among the geometric decorations on the pot. The silver saguaro with inset black ribs had the feel of a paperweight.

I admired the figurine. "What a treasure," I said. "Thank you."

"You won't let on where you got it, will you?"

"Absolutely not. Your secret is safe with me."

"I have a certain image to uphold. I better get back to my grandfather's room. Get well, Arizona Guy." He left quickly.

In the evening, Sandy called again. Her first words were, "Are you up for going to Colonia Morelos, Sonora, Mexico?"

"You found Aunt Betty and Uncle Bart!" I said.

"We found where we think they are. We'll have to check in person. There are no phones in the area."

"And obviously cell phones don't work. Well, I'm not doing much of anything the rest of the day," I said. "Let's go."

I told her I expected to be released in the morning. T.J. wandered in while we were talking and offered his RV. Sandy thought that was a good idea so I could lie down while we traveled. She said she would find a ride to the hospital. That way she wouldn't have to leave her car.

Sandy said, "You can rest easy tonight. We made an arrest in your assault case."

"Who was it?"

"Rodney Zamecki."

"Rodney Zamecki? Why did he do it? I haven't even met him."

"You're not going to believe this. You know that laugh box that woke you the other night?"

"I'm not believing it already."

"It actually belonged to Rodney. According to Rodney, Juan Rios borrowed it the day he set it off in school. Rodney made him steal it back. This time he lent it to Steve, and he wanted it back again."

"How did he know I had it?"

"Steve told him he left it by the closet door, so Rodney tried to get in through the basement—"

"After the lock was changed," I said.

"He was still in the area when you showed it to Marco. He saw you put it back in your pocket. He said he only gave you a tap with the shovel. He couldn't believe you were out cold."

"He doesn't know his own strength."

"Anyway, consider this your official victim notification. He'll be arraigned in the morning."

"I have more important fish to fry. Anyway, you're right."

"I'm right?"

"I don't believe his motive."

Sandy offered to pick up some clothing for me if she could get Manny to let her in the house.

"Hey, would you bring my flute, too?" I asked. "I'm going to need it."

"Okay."

I was glad she didn't ask why. I hadn't come up with a convincing lie.

It was another long night. Nurses woke me every hour, checking temperature, heart rate, oxygen saturation, and blood pressure. They took blood, changed IV bags, asked questions to make sure I really didn't have a concussion, and took more blood.

"Why do you need blood?" I asked. "I'm getting out in the morning."

The nurse said, "If we don't get blood, you don't get out."

"Take as much as you want."

I was dozing when a whisper woke me.

"Rats. We're too early."

I couldn't tell if it was male or female.

"Can't you wait a few minutes?"

That was female.

"Not really."

"Ellen's there."

"She needs to be back in Payson."

I opened my eyes. A lean, self-assured, honey-blond man stood beside the bed. "Scott," I said, my mouth sluggish with sleep.

"Good morning, Ted," he said. "Did we wake you?"

"Wake me?" I said. "It's morning."

"It's just as well. I brought Blanca so that I could thank you personally for your part in figuring out where my parents went."

"Aren't you coming to Colonia Morelos?"

"Someone needs to be in Ajo just in case they come back, and Ellen has to go back to Payson today."

"At least take the new house key," I said.

Scott shook my hand firmly, murmured more thanks, and soon took his leave to head back to Ajo.

I felt like singing as I took a shower and dressed in the sensible jeans and t-shirt Sandy brought.

Sandy said she had left my flute and additional clothing with T.J. She studied the saguaro cactus figurine. "Who brought you this?"

We had time to watch a local morning show before my discharge came through. No mention was made of the Cochise County fires, which we took to mean they were pretty much extinguished.

Sandy drove the first leg of the trip to Tucson while T.J. dozed in the back. Interstate 10 was packed with traffic, even halfway past Picacho Peak. We stopped for a quick take-out breakfast, hardly interrupting an enjoyable conversation. T.J. drove the rest of the trip. The leg to Benson, still on I-10, was short. The Whetstone fire had come near the freeway, and we caught glimpses of blackened slopes.

Leaving the freeway, we went through Tombstone, ignoring advertisements for the Gunfight at the O.K. Corral, before seeing up close the aftermath of the Toughnut Fire. The residue of flares on the pavement and barricades off to the side were signs that the highway had been closed while the fire raged. There followed ten miles of charred hillsides on both sides of the highway. The acrid smell of the fire seeped into the RV, despite closed windows and the filter of air conditioning. Yucca and mesquite stumps still emitted tendrils of smoke.

As we passed Bisbee, I looked for smoke from the Naco fire to the south, but none was visible. Reaching Douglas, we got in line to go into Mexico.

Sandy got out and talked to Mexican officials when we got to the Agua Prieta side of the border. I checked my watch. We had gotten here in just less than four hours. That was good time for the amount of traffic we had battled on the freeway. When she got back in, Sandy's eyebrows were scrunched together, creating three vertical lines in the middle of her forehead.

"What's the matter?" I asked.

"There's another fire. Right where we want to go. They said to avoid the area."

T.J. turned on the motor home and headed eastbound on the border highway. He said, "Do they have barricades set up?"

Sandy said, "They didn't say."

I said, "Drive around them if you have to, or find another way in. 'The way less traveled by.'"

"I don't think you understand," Sandy said. "Any way to Colonia Morelos is less traveled by. There are a few ranches in the area, but the colony was abandoned a century ago. There's just some skeletal buildings."

Soon we could see distant plumes of white smoke.

Sandy said, "They're not fighting the fire because there are no towns in its path. The ranches are mostly grassland." Awhile later she asked T.J. to slow down. "The turnoff should be right about here."

A pair of tire tracks no more visible than the road to Ellsworth ranch soon appeared on the right.

"That's it," said Sandy. "See the milepost?"

T.J. turned, slowing to a snail's pace. Rocks and ruts jolted the motor home.

"No barricades," said T.J. dodging a deep hole only to bounce over a large rock.

I said, "They're not needed. Only a madman would take a motor home on this road."

"Guilty as charged," said T.J.

Soon the road smoothed out and T.J. was able to drive somewhat faster.

We had entered a painting in a western art gallery. The dirt road meandered toward impressive blue mountains through yellow grassland, interspersed with thickets of green mesquite trees. With no wind, the only movement was the billowing smoke which dominated the scene.

I was worn out from all the travel. Sandy noticed and suggested I take a nap. She said it would still take several hours to reach our destination, which appeared to be about where the fire was most active.

I went back and stretched out on T.J.'s bed. I dropped right to sleep despite the unevenness of the dirt road. When I came back to the front, we were coming over a hill.

"You woke up just in time," Sandy said, pointing. "There it is."

I made out a blue RV, just like the one drawn by Manny Molina.

"We found them!" I said.

Suddenly, fire lit up the field behind the vehicle. Flames ran toward it. Four people emerged from a dilapidated building, ran pell-mell, and piled into the RV. The driver immediately floored it, but it took a moment for the RV to gain full speed. The range fire caught it. In a matter of seconds, like the pine tree I had seen so often on TV, the RV was fully engulfed, roiling in flames.

T.J. careened towards the burning RV, not seeming to realize the fire would catch us, too.

There was no escape from the oily black super-charged smoke pouring out of the roaring orange flames. I struggled to get out of the RV to save them. "Aunt Betty! Uncle Bart!" I yelled. "Aunt Betty! Uncle Bart!"

Chapter twenty-two

"It's okay. It's okay," said a familiar voice. I continued to thrash, trying to somehow save my family from the conflagration, but I couldn't get any closer. I was restrained by an unseen force.

"Wake up, Prince Charming. It's only a dream. It's okay."

My heart was pounding. I was drenched in sweat. The bed was a tangle of sheets where I had jumped around wildly. The soothing voice belonged to Sandy.

"What a nightmare," I said. "Are we there, yet?"

"We're getting close." Sandy sat on the edge of the bed. "What were you dreaming?"

"You don't want to know."

"Betty and Bart caught in the fire?"

"And two others. Are you a mind reader? You keep doing this."

"Bookbinder and Eddy?"

"Presumably. Nasty fire. It caught their motor home. Is there any chance that they escaped the fire?"

Sandy rested her cool hand on my arm. It had a calming influence.

She said, "Of course, there is. Fires don't burn everything in their path. They're capricious. They'll take out some trees and leave others, burn some homes and spare others, and leave entire swaths of grassland untouched."

"If Bart and Betty even came here—and all we have is circumstantial evidence—they may have gotten the records and gotten out before the fire hit."

"Some circumstantial evidence is very strong, as when you find a trout in the milk."

I stared at her. "Have you lost your marbles?"

"It's from Thoreau. If the farmer diluted milk with water that he dipped out of a spring you might—"

"—find a trout in the milk. Makes sense."

Sandy stood, withdrawing her hand from my arm. "In about ten minutes we should be pretty close." She ducked out of the tiny bedroom.

"'Prince Charming?'" I called.

Sandy ducked her head back in the doorway. "My mother always called me Sleeping Beauty when I had bad dreams. You're definitely not a Sleeping Beauty."

Sandy returned to the front passenger seat.

I made the bed, washed my face, and ran a comb through my hair. When I sat down behind Sandy, we were passing blackened grassland on both sides of the road, but the fire here was out.

I said, "Have we passed any buildings yet?"

T.J. said, "Not yet, but if the mileage figure Sandy got is accurate, we have another three miles."

We climbed a hill. Suddenly we were back in yellow grassland untouched by the fire.

Sandy said, "Do you suppose that the colony was spared?"

T.J. drove slowly over the crest. The burn line was

right where the road started descending.

Sandy said, "Oh, no."

Then I saw it, too. The valley beyond was all blackened. Eight or ten heaps of smoking rubble dotted the area.

I said, "I don't see any intact buildings."

Sandy said, "At least the fire isn't active here now."

"Look toward those blue mountains to the left. That's where it's still burning," T.J. said.

I said, "Do you see any sign of the blue RV Manny Molina drew?"

There was no sign of any living thing. The entire valley had been burned. We didn't see any places that had been missed.

"This fire must be the reason Betty and Bart didn't wait for you, Ted. Surely they saved the records and got out before it got here," Sandy said.

T.J. said, "If they didn't, there are no records left now."

"Spared for a hundred years, and then…." Sandy said.

I was sickened by the sight of so much devastation.

Sandy suddenly pointed ahead. "Stop, T.J. That's right in the road!"

One of the piles of smoking rubble blocked the road, giving off black smoke. No one said a word as we approached. T.J. came to a stop behind the remains of a large vehicle, at least as large as T.J.'s RV.

We all got out. T.J. walked all the way around it, while Sandy and I just gazed at the wreckage. The silence stretched out, almost tangible, as if no one wanted to admit the truth. No one even wanted to breathe. Blackened metal was distorted into impossible shapes, like those in an impressionistic painting depicting the horrors of war.

T.J. suddenly spoke, his voice loud after so long a silence. "It was a cattle truck. Look at the siding. You can see the panels with holes for air circulation and the solid panels for reinforcing. And there are regularly spaced girders for extra strength. You can tell it is much stronger than an RV. Plus I don't see the remnants of a stove or refrigerator. It was a cattle truck."

"You're right," Sandy said. I could hear relief in her voice.

I said, pointing, "That was the motor and that was the cab."

We were reassured enough to get back in the RV.

T.J. found a way around the burned-out wreck where there were no hot spots, and we were soon going again. Further along, we passed the largest building we had thus far seen. Smoke seemed to boil more actively than from the other ruins. As it was right beside the road, and we were so high in the RV, we could see that most of the smoke was coming from the cellar, which was now open to the sky.

"The fire down there isn't just smoldering. It's more active. There must be a lot to burn," Sandy said.

Soon we were beyond all the burned buildings and T.J. said, "Well, what do you think? We're leaving Colonia Morelos. Keep going or turn back?"

"Keep going," Sandy and I said as one.

Sandy said, "If they had gone back, surely we would have made contact."

As we came over the rise leaving the Colonia Morelos valley, we came back into yellow grassland. The road wound up at a small ranch house. There, in plain sight by the house, was the large blue RV Manny had drawn. It was larger than the house. A tent was pitched nearby.

The sound of a generator replaced the silence we had traveled through since leaving the highway.

"It's them," said Sandy. She reached back and gripped my hand, her eyes straight ahead.

"It has to be," I said.

Still, we didn't see any people. As we approached the RV door I noted a wheelchair lift at the far end. Sandy knocked. A lady's voice said, "Come in."

A gray-haired lady with thick glasses peered at us as we entered. Surrounded by huge wooden crates, cardboard boxes, and books, she was seated at a computer which looked suspiciously like Uncle Bart's. I had never seen her before.

"Yes?" she said, tapping her closely trimmed nails, looking furtively back at the computer monitor. Then I noticed she was in a wheelchair. A pair of crutches leaned against the wall.

"We're looking for Betty and Bart Ellsworth," I blurted.

"I think they're over at the house." She shrugged and started typing again.

We introduced ourselves, but the gray-haired lady never looked up again and didn't reply. I led the way to the house and knocked. There was a whisper of movement inside. The door opened, and I was again looking at someone I didn't know, heavyset, Hispanic, elderly with long white hair. I introduced us and asked about Bart and Betty. She didn't say a word.

Sandy stepped forward and spoke rapid Spanish. "Sí," said the lady. That was the only word I understood in a torrent of Spanish. She stood back for us to enter. The living room was empty of people, but voices came from a bedroom.

Aunt Betty, Uncle Bart, and the balding man with a mustache Manny had drawn were all in the bedroom surrounding a mother and very tiny baby, only a few days old.

Uncle Bart came out, a quizzical expression on his lined, clean-shaven face. "Ted, Sandy, T.J.? Is there a problem?"

I rushed forward. "You're okay! You're all okay!"

Bart enfolded me in an embrace. "Of course we're okay. Why wouldn't we be?"

Suddenly I was in tears. I couldn't believe the sense of release at finding them safe. Bart let go of me and I found myself in Betty's arms. I couldn't shake the tears. Sandy got the same treatment, first by Bart and then by Betty. T.J. stood back grinning.

I shook the hand of the balding man with the mustache.

Bart said, "This is David Bookbinder. His wife is in the RV."

My head whirling, I also met Ramona Nuñez and cooed over her baby. Ramona's mother, Tomasa Obregon, disappeared into the kitchen.

We found places to sit in the living room before I finally was able to speak.

"The reason we tracked you down was to make sure you're all right. You disappeared without a trace and we thought something bad had happened."

Betty said, "Why? Didn't you know where we went?"

T.J., Sandy, and I all shook our heads.

Betty said, looking at me, "How can that be? I left you a message on your phone, a note on the door, and I told Gladys. I tried to reach your cell phone, but it wasn't available."

I said to Betty, "When did you leave the phone message?"

"Tuesday morning when all our plans changed."

I said, "I left Monday. I never got the message. The note disappeared, and poor Gladys Takamine had a TIA."

Betty said, "What's a TIA?"

I said, "A Transient Ischemic Attack. A piece of plaque from one of her arteries broke off and traveled through the part of her brain that controls memory. She never remembered what you told her. And still doesn't, even though she has recovered."

"Poor Gladys," said Betty.

Bart nodded. "But I still don't understand why you were so worried," he said. "It seems all out of proportion for being gone a few days."

I said, "Sandy, why don't you tell them the rest of the story?"

Sandy did.

Betty and Bart looked at each other in amazement. They were speechless.

Sandy said, "And then the cooler was vandalized...."

Bart said, "I see why you were worried. Is there a house left?"

"Yes," I said. "T.J. rekeyed the house and repaired the cooler. The house is fine."

Sandy said, "And then Ted fell off the roof, got whacked by a shovel, and fell into a coma due to electrolyte depletion..."

"A coma!" gasped Betty.

"They put me back together in the hospital and let me out this morning."

Betty said with finality, "Then you've done enough

traveling for one day. Don't even consider going back to Ajo until tomorrow."

"Yes, Aunty Mother," I said, drawing laughs.

Bart said, "Our story pales by comparison. The only excitement other than finding the lost records was the fire. It blocked us from leaving, so we came here to the Rancheria Obregon for refuge."

"And we got to help Ramona have her baby. The fire blocked the road to the hospital," Betty said.

I turned to David Bookbinder. "I don't understand why you needed help. Why didn't you throw the records in the RV and bring them to Ajo?"

"Most of the records are in huge crates. It took three of us to get some of them out of that cellar," David said.

"Couldn't someone here help you?"

"You've met my wife. Ramona was about to give birth. Her parents are too old and feeble. Her husband is away. There was no one else."

"What about Eddy? Why couldn't he help?"

David smiled. "Eddy is my wife, short for Eduvijen. Her name got her interested in genealogy."

"She's one of the best in the world. A cryptic reference in St. George led her here. Just before the records would have been destroyed," added Bart.

I wasn't satisfied. "Why didn't you take the papers out of the crates...?"

Bart interrupted, "You don't give up, do you?"

"That's why we found you," Sandy said.

"After a hundred years, the paper is really brittle. Too much handling would have destroyed the records," David said.

I had another question. "How did you know about the fire?"

David said, "Ramona's father, Jose Obregon, reached us by ham radio. He said we had time to get to Ajo and back."

Uncle Bart said, "More to the point, how did you find us, if none of Betty's messages reached you?"

I said, "Does Disc J ring a bell? Why did you store it in the refrigerator?"

Uncle Bart said, "Oh, that's why you asked about Eddy. Years ago I lost a back-up disc when there was a power outage and it got too hot. I found Disc J still in the office when I was doing a last-minute check before locking up, so I tossed it in the coldest drawer I could think of. But how did it benefit you? I had the computer."

I said, "Another prank helped us find the basement which had your back-up computer."

Bart said, "How many pranks were there?"

"I stopped counting."

I asked about the golden retrievers. "I thought you were planning to leave them home."

"We were," said Bart, "until we decided to travel in style. When we got to the Douglas area, David suddenly wondered about bringing dogs back from Mexico. So we enquired, and found that they would have to be quarantined for several weeks."

Betty said, "We left them with friends in Douglas."

After dark I went out to stretch my legs, feeling at peace and well on the way to a total recovery from the electrolyte problem. The stars were more numerous than I had ever seen, despite smoke on the horizon. I leaned against the top rail of the corral gazing up at the living, pulsating night sky. No planes. No flares. The moon hadn't risen yet, so the stars were especially vivid. The Milky Way was splashed diagonally across the sky.

I thought about all that had happened since I drove out of Greenwood City with such conflicted emotions. My biggest question then was whether I should sign my contract to teach in Greenwood City. I still didn't have an answer, and now I had a second contract offer to teach in Ajo.

Suddenly I knew my answer. People. I had been in Ajo only a short time, but I had people there I cared about more than anyone in Greenwood City. In California I had acquaintances. In Ajo I had friends. As I stood by the corral on the Rancheria Obregon in northern Mexico looking into the heavens, the conviction rose in my heart that Ajo was the right place for me.

Aunt Betty and Uncle Bart came out of their tent and found me gazing upward quite awhile later.

Betty said, "Thank you for caring enough to track us down. I'm sorry for failing to get word to you when we left. Once we got here, we were totally involved, but I could have tried harder on the way."

"Who knew your messages would be lost?" I said. "But it worked out for the best. I've been standing here thinking about all the people I've gotten close to in Ajo, and it's because you were missing. I've gotten my answer. I'm going to accept Bishop Reynolds' offer to teach in Ajo."

Uncle Bart said, "You have made a wise decision. Taking the Ajo position won't be the easiest challenge of your life, but it will be the best."

Back in T.J.'s RV, Sandy had taken the bedroom, leaving T.J. and me the living room with its sofa and soft carpet. I brought out my flute and began to clean it. Sandy came out, ready for bed, and watched for a moment.

I looked up. "I made my decision," I said.

"What does your heart tell you?" She closed her eyes as if wishing on a star.

"To take the music position in Ajo."

Sandy opened her eyes. "Did you just say you were going to take the music position in Ajo, or was I just wishing it?"

"Both," I said.

Sandy's smile broadened and her dimple threatened to become permanent. She closed her eyes for a moment. "Wise choice."

"That's what Uncle Bart said."

"Oh, so you didn't tell me first. I see where I rate." But she never lost her dimple.

I fitted the flute together and finished polishing it.

"So that's a flute," Sandy said impishly.

"How many years has it been?" I asked.

"Too many to even think about it," she said, but her dimple said otherwise.

"See if you can at least produce a note," I coaxed.

She hesitantly took it, but she couldn't get her embouchure right.

"You're smiling too much," I said.

She tried again and played a B-flat major scale perfectly.

I said, "I promise not to keep trying to repay you for everything you've done for me this last week if you'll take this instrument off my hands and join the community band."

"It's a deal," she said, looking me in the eye. She lifted the flute back to her lips and played.

***

CPSIA information can be obtained
at www.ICGtesting.com
Printed in the USA
JSHW031129061220
10056JS00001B/15